BALLAD OF A FORBIDDEN HOOD AFFAIR 2

EUPHORIA & LYNX STORY

AKIRE C.

Published by S.Yvonne Presents

❀ Created with Vellum

SUBSCRIBE

Interested in keeping up with more releases from S.Yvonne Presents? To be notified first of all upcoming releases, exclusive sneak peaks, and contest to win prizes. Please subscribe to her mailing list by texting Syvonnepresents to 22828

This book is dedicated to Chimere (My headache), Tyanna (My boo), and Lexi B (Lil baby) without y'all this book probably wouldn't have gotten finished. As much as I was doubting myself and was constantly in my head y'all gave me rock solid feedback every single time. Thank y'all soooooooooooooo much!

Every woman deserves a man who writes poems on her body with his lips. And every man deserves a woman who craves his touch.

~Mardy Bryant~

KEEP IN TOUCH WITH ME

Please feel free to connect with me on the following social media platforms:
Facebook Reader's Group: AkireC's Reading Addicts

FACEBOOK: AKIRE C. AUTHOR

FACEBOOK AUTHOR PAGE: AUTHOR AKIRE C.

Twitter: @akirec_author
Instagram: author_akire_c
TikTok: author_akire_c

SYNOPSIS

Euphoria is a headstrong Taurus who was determined to get her man and she successfully succeeded the feat. Though the task was not as challenging as she'd thought it would be, everything that happened between them was next level. The bond and connection they developed was so deep and intense at times it was scary.

Lynx didn't stand a chance going up against temptation and losing. He found himself not only filling a void but finding his soulmate, the one he believed was specifically created for him. Juvie, as he affectionately calls her, is a force to be reckoned with as she captures his heart and imprints his soul. Her position is pretty much solidified in his life but he's still harboring a dark secret that could potentially destroy everything they've built.

As we all know when things are going too good, something bad is usually lurking in the shadows waiting to rear its ugly head. There will be even more secrets revealed, unexpected connections, plot twists you never saw coming, and most importantly you'll find out who's at the door.

INTERLUDE:

I Feel Good All Over By: Stephanie Mills

PREVIOUSLY

I'm Trapped
Lynx Malveaux

It had been almost two weeks since Juvie and I went out of town for her birthday and her graduation was literally days away. I can't lie that was one of the best times I've ever had in my life. She went to her prom the weekend before last and she didn't even stay the whole time. She may have been there an hour before calling me to come get her and I did. Her lil spoiled ass got me wrapped around her finger but that's gonna be my baby forever.

Juvie just don't know she stuck with a nigga, and I don't even think I have control of the situation. Our souls have tied which only solidified our bond and deepened our connection. I don't think she knows the severity of what we've done. She's been reading up on it and researching like I'd asked her to do and is very intrigued with what she's learning. I just hope she understands that's why I'm gonna forever be on her ass like white on rice, which is why I'm headed to her house right now before I go to work. Her last day of school was this past Tuesday and I've stopped here three mornings this week. I had been leaving the house earlier than usual just so I can drop LuLu off to daycare, go by Juvie once her mama leave, and still make sure my ass gets to work on time.

Me: *Good Morning love, I'm on my way to you now.*

Juvie: Good Morning baby. Come on, I'm up cooking, and they're already gone.

Me: Ok. I'll be there in a few minutes.

Juvie: Can't wait.

I texted Juvie to let her know I was on my way just to make sure the coast was clear before I pulled up. She still hasn't told her folks about me, and I'm cool with that considering my situation at home. Once I made it on her street, I made the block before finally pulling in just in case her mama doubled back and came home for something, never putting any thought into the possibility of her doubling back once I was inside. When it comes to Juvie my thought process isn't always rational and more so on a deal with a situation if one presents itself. I got out and knocked on the door so she could let me in. She opened the door with a short silk robe tied at the waist that had a nigga already drooling and bricking up in my work pants.

"Morning baby." She greeted me with a wide smile and a soft kiss on the lips. "I cooked breakfast for you. Do you wanna eat first?"

"Damn it smells good but check it let me deal with you first and I'll deal with that after."

"Ok daddy!" She replied sauntering over to the stove making sure it was turned off before grabbing my hand and leading me to her bedroom.

She undid the belt on her robe exposing the Chinese baroque print lingerie gown she was wearing underneath it and tossing it aside. The navy blue, white, and gold colors were vibrant and looked amazing against her skin causing my dick to spring to life. I couldn't get out of my work clothes fast enough but when I did it was on. I picked her up and she instinctively wrapped her legs around my waist. The warmth from her bare pussy caused my dick to jump and repeatedly tap on her lips. I laid her on her back taking in her beauty as she stared back at me with those sexy ass cat eyes. Without breaking eye contact with me she rose up pulling the gown over her head throwing it beside her, so she was now just as naked as me. Her hardened nipples stood at attention causing my mouth to water. I hovered over her allowing the pre-cum oozing from my dick to tease her clit and her face began to contort with pure gratification. I began to kiss, lightly nibble, blow, and suck on her nipples providing them each with an equivalent amount of pleasure until her body began to writhe uncontrollably beneath me. Our connection was so deep I could literally make her cum without even penetrating her, but I was pushed for time, so I didn't want her to cum just yet. Leaning over the bed respecting her request, I retrieved the condom from my pants pocket. Tearing it open I rolled it on my dick before spreading her legs east and west.

"You ready for me lil mama?" I questioned while positioning the head at the entrance of my favorite place and she nodded.

Another thing I loved about Juvie is the fact that her pussy is always tight and juicy for a nigga. I started inching my way inside allowing her walls to suffocate my dick. Once I was all the way in, I laid in the pussy until she had adjusted to me. I had her legs spread wide in the air about to go to work when she removed my grip from the left one slipping it behind her head with a wicked grin spread across her face.

"Fuck Juvie!" I groaned out in amazement that she was able to comfortably do that with my dick deep inside of her. I began with a slow grind deep in that pussy making sure to hit each and every one of her spots.

"Oooohhhhh! Fuck, you in my stomach." She moaned out with so much passion I swear my dick did the impossible and got even harder.

"You want me to stop?" I asked considering the size of my dick and the position she was in a nigga might just be putting pressure on her stomach.

"You wanna die?" She replied cocking her head to the side and I shook my head no. She freed her other leg from my grip putting it behind her head as well. This fucking girl here is too damn flexible for her own good. "Awww fuck! Yes, right there! Please don't fucking stop!" I had to look away because she was about to make me nut and I needed her to get hers first.

I started going crazy in the pussy and it was talking back to me. Juvie's moans plus the sound of her pussy farting was about to make a nigga explode.

"Juvie stop tryna hold it and cum for me."

"Oooohhhhh Lynx, right there! Don't stop right fucking there." She growled at me and that shit kinda turned me on. She pulled her legs from behind her head and secured them around my waist and pulled me in even deeper. I leaned down tracing her lip with my tongue because she liked it when I did that before plunging it into her mouth. Our tongues wrestled with each other as I continued drilling into her and hitting her spot as she requested. All of a sudden, her eyes stretched wide, catching me off guard. I broke our kiss and pulled out of her thinking I was hurting her something. What happened next was the complete opposite she started squirting and wetting me up like a fire hydrant that was opened for the kids in the projects to play in on a hot summer day.

"Ahhhhhhhhhh Lynx!" She moaned as she rode out the waves of her orgasm. "That was everything!"

"Yeah, it was you'll be changing your sheets in a minute." I said looking down at the large puddle she had made. "Come on and turnover for me love?"

Once she had caught her breath, she rolled over getting in the doggy style position. She had her face buried in the pillow with her ass hoisted in the perfect arch. I had to bite my fist to prevent me from screaming like a lil bitch. Her long hair hung loosely down her back, and I gathered a handful as I slid back in her pussy effortlessly. I was literally knee deep in the pussy, with a fistful of her hair beating the pussy up when she started throwing it back on a nigga. She was moaning into the pillow as my balls repeatedly slapped against her pussy with each stroke. I could feel my nut building up and I started rotating my hips and slowing my stroke into a nice lil slow grind.

"Fuck Juvie! I'm bout to bust!" I growled damn near out of breath as she was clenching her pussy muscles around my dick trying to pull the nut out. Juvie's pussy is so good with and without a rubber, definitely like sunshine on a cloudy day, I thought just as I bust a huge nut filling up the rubber. I carefully pulled my dick out, so I didn't spill any of my kids inside of her even though I wouldn't mind if I did. It was at that moment I decided I wanted Juvie to have my baby one day, I thought as I got up to go to the bathroom. I pulled the rubber off and flushed it down the toilet before grabbing the towel she already had waiting for me to wash up. She was coming into the bathroom to pee just as I was finishing up. I tossed the towel in the hamper in the bathroom closet and went back in her room to get redressed for work.

"You want me to warm your plate up so you can eat

before you leave?" She asked coming into the room drying her hands on a towel.

"Yeah, can you put it on a paper plate so I can take it with me love?" I requested after looking at my watch and seeing the time.

"Of course. Plus, I know you gotta get to work." She stated slipping her robe back on and I looked away in an effort to keep my dick from getting back hard.

"What you got up for today?" I asked, trailing her to the kitchen.

"Rissa and I are supposed to go looking for our graduation dresses and shoes this morning and we got work later but that's about it."

Once she had warmed my food up and transferred it to a to-go box she passed it to me. She grabbed plastic utensils, napkins, and a bottle of Tropicana orange juice, passing it to me. "Let me get outta here before I'm late. I'll be there to scoop you from work later, love you Juvie."

"Ok baby, I love you too! See you later." She replied before kissing me and opening the door to let me out.

I got in my truck and quickly got situated so I could eat and drive. No wonder this food smelled good it looks good too. My baby made a nigga cheese grits, scrambled eggs, bacon, and a fluffy buttermilk biscuit that she had spread evenly with mixed fruit jelly. I swear this girl never ceases to amaze me. I honestly was starting to wish I had met her before saying I do to Miranda. A nigga really out here living the lyrics of that blues song, *Trapped* by Carl Sims. He ain't never lied when he said, *"I don't know what to do. I'm so in love with the two. Jumping in and outta bed is messing with my head. I don't know, I don't know what to do."*

I took a scoop of grits and eggs stuffing it into my mouth and had to close my eyes for a second as I savored the flavor.

This was some of the best breakfast food I'd ever had, and I couldn't wait to see what else she could whip up in the kitchen, I thought before pulling off. Juvie was right on time with that food she must've known a nigga's energy was gonna be depleted fucking with her flexible ass. Damn shame I get better sex from an eighteen-year-old then I do my damn wife. I often find myself comparing the two and no lie when it comes to Juvie, Miranda can't even compete where she doesn't compare. Juvie is something serious and every man deserves a fucking Juvie, just not mine though.

As I was driving my mind wandered off back to the encounter with Slugga when Rissa got sick or whatever happened to her. I hadn't heard anything as of yet, so I guess it was safe to say the lil nigga ain't snitched me out to Miranda yet. I know him from dating and having a baby with one of Miranda's nieces. Shit, to be honest I thought they were still together but then again, I don't really know or see them like that to be caught up on their relationship status. From what I knew he was smart as a whip and his daddy and mama had big bread, so I was totally baffled as to why he was trying to get involved in this street shit as he mentioned that day at his house. I don't understand why these youngin's wanna be in the streets when they have no reason too, I thought shaking my head as I continued driving. I pulled into work just as I finished the last piece of my biscuit. A nigga could really use a nap right now, but I had to shake that shit off and get ready to handle my route.

Work literally flew by today which doesn't happen too often. Checking the time, I realized I had a little over an hour or so before I needed to pick LuLu from daycare. I was bobbing my head to Lil Flip's *Game Over* one of Juvie's favorite songs. She loves her some Lil Flip hell she loves music period which is another connection we have between us. We literally can find a song for us to zone out and be in our own little bubble. I pulled in my driveway and rolled a joint to smoke. Once I was higher than an electric bill in the south during the summer, I rolled the windows down and sprayed my truck letting it air out. After about ten minutes, I rolled the windows up and got out to head inside and shower. Not even five minutes later there was a series of loud knocks on the door, which raised a red flag, and I knew I wasn't expecting anyone. I grabbed my gun and making sure one was in the chamber, I aimed the gun prepared to take a shot if needed when I swung the door open. I wasn't sure if I should be shocked, upset or pissed at the person staring back at me who didn't appear to be fazed at all about the gun pointed directly at their forehead.

"What the fuck are you doing here?" I questioned as my unexpected visitor stood there with a smug grin plastered on their face.

EVERYTHING

LYNX MALVEAUX

"Sup Lynx?" My unexpected visitor replied holding his fist out for me to dap him down.

"Jahziah or is it Slugga now? What the fuck are you doing just popping up unannounced at my crib like this?" I seethed and I could feel the smoke coming from my head. I was hotter than grease at a Friday night fish fry.

"It ain't what you think bruh. Can I just holla at ya for a minute?"

"You got two minutes to state your business and get the fuck off my property." I let the nigga know as I stepped outside pulling the door behind me holding my glock by my side.

"First off, I just wanna say whatever you got going on with E ain't my business and you ain't gotta worry about me saying anything. If I'm being honest y'all look good together besides, I never liked that bitch Mir-" was all he managed to get out before I slapped the fuck outta him with the butt of the gun.

"Watch ya mouth nigga that's still my wife."

"My fault." He responded while moving his jaw around

checking to see if I broke anything. "I know you get down in the streets and I just wanna see if you can put me on."

"Nigga I don't what kinda FED shit you on, but I work for UPS. You know the ones with the doodoo brown uniform."

"Come on man, I know you moving work in the streets."

"Get the fuck outta my face and outta my driveway before shit turn out bad for you." I told him in a voice so cold a chill ran down my own damn spine.

He stared at me for a few seconds before turning on his heels. One thing I can say is when I looked in his eyes, I didn't see fear, just determination. I wonder if his reason for not mentioning my relationship with Juvie was him proving his loyalty or an attempt to blackmail me to get what he wants. Hopefully, it ain't the latter cause I would hate to have to put a hot one in his ass.

After making sure that nigga was gone, I went back inside so I could shower and get myself together to go get LuLu. Once I had showered and put on some lotion, I got dressed in a black t-shirt, black and red basketball shorts, socks, and my black and red Air Max, finishing it off with my matching Nike snapback. I grabbed my wallet and keys and made my way out the house locking up behind me, I hopped in my truck and headed to the daycare. It took me about ten minutes to get there and I went inside to sign baby girl out. After checking the time, I knew Miranda most likely still hadn't made it home yet to cook and a nigga was high and hungry as fuck. So, it wasn't rocket-science for me to go by my baby's job since I hadn't seen her since this morning.

The drive-thru line was long as hell when I pulled into Juvie's job. I parked and grabbed a giggling LuLu out the back before going inside. Shit they were short staffed like a muthafucka which explained the long ass line outside. It was only Juvie, Rissa, one nigga in the back and whoever the shift manager was must've been in the office, so I took a seat and waited til they slowed down to place my order. A nigga was thirty-eight hot when I realized my baby and Rissa was taking orders and making them too instead of the manager coming out and helping them, I bet it's that bitch I dissed that be hating. I was pissed but at the same time in awe cause they was handling that shit and in no time they had handled all of the customers inside and outside. Getting up I approached the front counter where Rissa was standing, finally ready to place my order.

"Sup Rissa?" I greeted her as I stared over in Juvie's direction, she was stocking cups in the drive-thru. The way her ass was sitting in them uniform pants had a nigga ready to pin her ass up right where she was and put this dick on her.

"Hi sir, may I take your order?" Rissa replied confirming my suspicions of which manager was on duty otherwise she would have said something different.

"Yeah, let me get a nugget Happy Meal with Sprite mixed with water and a medium number one with a Coke easy ice."

"Sure. Is that for here or to go?"

"Here." I replied just as Juvie walked up.

"Hey baby." She spoke with a warm smile and LuLu started reaching for her.

"Sup love?" I replied licking my lips as I stared into her eyes while she tickled LuLu.

"Don't you start." She gave me the side eye cause she knew where my mind was headed.

"I'm good cause now ain't the time or place to get myself all riled up. Did y'all get everything handled for tomorrow?"

"Yep, I can't wait for you to see me in my lil dress. Are you still coming tomorrow?"

"I wouldn't miss seeing you walk across that stage for nothing in the world."

"We still linking up after?"

"Most definitely! Ya know I gotta give you your gift." I winked confirming our plans just as Rissa placed my tray on the counter. I walked LuLu to the table and placed her in the highchair before going back and grabbing our food and drinks.

"I'm sure there is some work y'all could be doing." That bitch yelled from the back which had me fuming and ready to address it. If it wasn't for Juvie's eyes pleading with me to let it go I was definitely about to let her ass have it. I nodded letting her know I would and focused on setting up LuLu's food for her before digging into my own. While eating, I stole glances at Juvie, shit it was hard not to with them damn uniform pants on.

After we were done eating, I cleaned LuLu's hands and mouth before throwing our trash away and putting the tray up. I opened her toy and gave it to her before picking her up from the highchair and pushing it aside I walked up to the front to holler at my baby before I bounced.

"Lil Mama I'm bout to head home but I'll be back later to pick you up."

"Ok baby, see you then." She replied blowing me a kiss. "Love you."

"Love you too." I responded with a wink before turning and leaving out.

Once I had LuLu strapped in her car seat and I was behind the wheel, we headed home. Miranda's truck was parked under the carport and for some reason my whole mood changed. Lately, things have been rocky and that's why I prefer to be in the streets even more when I'm not with

Juvie. I sighed before finally getting out and grabbing LuLu and going inside.

"Sup y'all?" I spoke to her and LJ at the same time since they were both in the dining room. She was helping him with his homework and cooking at the same time.

"Hey babe." She responded dryly and I was fine with that.

"Sup dad?" LJ greeted me with his fist pointed and I bumped it before passing LuLu to Miranda.

"You almost done with your homework?"

"Yes sir." I nodded and made my way down the hall to use the bathroom.

After I finished pissing, I washed my hands and walked outta the bathroom to Miranda sitting on the bed with LuLu. Here goes the bullshit I thought to myself as I tried to read her facial expression to see what she was on.

"Where have you been?" I looked around to see if there was somebody else in the room cause I know damn well she ain't questioning me.

"Excuse me?" I asked just to make sure I wasn't tripping.

"Well, I didn't know you was picking Lynexia up until I got to the daycare and saw that you had already signed her out. It's obvious you didn't come straight home."

"And your point?"

"Why are you so defensive, you act like I accused you of cheating?"

"I ain't defensive about shit. I'm just trying to understand the point of you so-called questioning me like I'm not a grown man."

"And I'm just trying to figure out where have you been with my child?"

"I know damn well you ain't just say your child like you laid there and made her by your damn self." I was livid at this point, and it was best that I get the hell outta here before I say some shit I regret. I stormed past her without so much as a see ya later.

"Lynx so you're just gonna ignore me and walk away like I'm not talking to you." I abruptly stopped walking and she was so close that she ran into my back. I turned around and glared at her because for one she was holding LuLu and two LJ was a few feet away in the dining room and this shit was not about to take place in front of my kids. I continued my trek to the door with her still on my heels, stopping next to her truck.

"Miranda, I don't know what you're on, but you know I don't do this in front of my kids and definitely not outside. I strongly suggest you turn around and take my baby back inside."

"So instead of answering my question you're gonna leave like it's not time for dinner. I found a new recipe and worked hard on that shrimp pasta." By this point I was fuming yeah, I need to get the fuck on down before I say some shit that I may or may not regret.

"I'm leaving because I'm a man and I don't owe you no explanations about my whereabouts. As for that recipe, if you hadn't already pissed me off placing a plate of shrimp pasta would have definitely done it. I'm starting to think you tryna take a nigga out since you love cooking shit, I'm allergic too." I left her standing there with her mouth on the floor and her eyes stretched wide when I called her out on her bullshit. I got in my truck and waited until she took her simple ass back inside before pulling off with no particular destination in mind.

I drove around aimlessly before I knew it, I was pulling up to the liquor store a nigga definitely needed a bottle. If I would have known shit would have turned out I like this, I would have Supersized my damn food. I got me a lil pint of

Paul Masson, a can of crunk juice, and a cup of ice. Once I paid for my shit I got in my truck and mixed my drink up and threw the bottle and shit away before pulling off and heading to my next destination. I had more than enough time to grab something to eat, make a few sells and shit before it was time for me to go get Juvie from work.

As I cruised through the streets my mind drifted back to Slugga and him wanting to be put on. I still wasn't sure if I wanted to fuck with him like that or not but the lil nigga had heart and I could tell he was hungry. It was definitely in his eyes that he really wanted in on this street shit, but I gotta really put some thought into if I really wanna fuck with him like that. One wrong move could cost me my life, either hell or jail and if I could help it I ain't going out like that, I thought as I pulled up to my lil trap spot.

I LOVE ME SOME HIM

EUPHORIA GUIDRY

It is officially graduation day. I'm up getting ready because Rissa will be here soon so we can go to graduation rehearsal. We had gone to get our nails and toes done at Guarantee Nails on Plank Road yesterday instead of trying to go today. My nails and toes were designed with black, white, and gold while Rissa opted for black, white, and red. We finished in time to stop and grab lunch before we headed to our hair appointments at Klassy Styles so Torsor could hook up our hair. Since, we gotta wear them damn graduation caps we both chose to get our hair bone straight and let her wrap it up for us until today, so it won't get frizzy. We're still keeping our hair wrapped up til the actual ceremony, so I made sure my wrap cap was secured before covering it with my Jordan snapback. I was rocking a pair of denim shorts, a pink and white Jordan t-shirt, paired with the white, pink, and metallic silver low Jordan 12s that came out last week. Just as I was glossing my lips, I heard Rissa honking her horn. After giving myself a quick once over I hurriedly made my way outside before Rissa started honking again and woke up the whole damn neighborhood.

"Heyyyyy friend!" I greeted Rissa as soon as I got in the car.

"Heyyyy bitch!" She replied all cheerful and shit.

Since she still hadn't mentioned anything about what landed her in the hospital, and I had been trying to give her time to process whatever it was and tell me. Today I'm gonna address it because she is not only my best friend, but my sister and she should know she can come to me and I'm gonna support her no matter what. We don't keep secrets and I've respected her privacy long enough. Shit she still hasn't told her parents she was in the hospital.

"Friend?" I started before turning the music down.

"What's up?"

"You ready to tell me what landed you in the hospital?" Peeping the sudden change in her body language she let out a dramatic sigh.

"I'm pregnant friend." She answered as tears suddenly slid down her cheeks.

"Rissa pull over." I instructed so that I could calm her down before she killed us in an accident. "Calm down and take a deep breath for me."

"Like how the fuck did this shit even happen?" She started followed by another dramatic sigh. "I always made sure Brandon strapped up just to prevent some shit like this from happening."

"So, y'all ain't never had any slip-ups ever?"

"No, I would have remembered something like that?"

"Well, how the fuck you get knocked up cause you damn sure ain't The Virgin Mary?"

"I have no idea unless that muthafucka put holes in them or was taking them off!!" She seethed with her chest heaving. "I'm gonna kill him."

"Rissa calm down and stop being so damn dramatic. You

can't kill him, so you need to tell him, your parents, and just go from there." I tried to be the voice of reason. "Does Slugga know?" I noticed her body tense up out of my peripheral.

"It's not what you think." She started as I peered over at her causing her to sweat as she provided an explanation as to why Slugga knew before me. After she explained that he was actually suggesting she take a pregnancy test just before she had the dizzy spell and passed out which is how she ended up in the hospital, I cut her some slack. It was more so he was in the right place at the right time, I'm just glad my girl is good.

"OMG!" I screamed once our conversation had finally registered.

"What the fuck is wrong with you, E?"

"I'm gonna be an auntie duh."

"Here we go, and I haven't even decided what I wanna do yet?" I stared a hole in the side of her head as she put the car in drive and continued the short ride to Bethany Church where our graduation will be held. "I feel you staring at me, and I didn't mean it like that. I was just saying what if I decide to put the baby up for adoption?"

"Girl boom! You know damn well you ain't giving no baby away."

"Yeah, you probably right but the million-dollar question is do I really wanna be bothered with Brandon for the next eighteen years?"

"Yikes the price to pay for being a slut." I replied with a giggle.

"If that ain't the pot calling the kettle black. I know you ain't talking as much as Lynx be tickling your tonsils and shit."

"And do!"

"Y'all asses are nasty! What are y'all gonna do if Ms. Karla catch y'all fucking in her house?"

"Shit, finish." I replied hunching my shoulders.

"Yo' ass is crazy." Rissa had briefly put me in my head considering the risk our asses be taking damn near every morning. To be honest, if we were to get caught the only thing she could do is bitch about us doing the shit in her house other than that I'm grown. Besides, we be doing it in his mama house too, no mama house left behind.

"I still can't believe in just a few short hours we will be high school graduates." I stated as Rissa and I walked to her car. We had just finished rehearsal and really didn't have anything to do so we were heading to her house.

"I know right. Then it's off to college in the fall. We bout to be hitting the college parties and everything." Rissa responded and hi-fived me before starting the car and pulling off.

"Yes, I can't wait to experience college life. Friend how you gonna be partying with a big belly?" I managed to get out just as I got a text from my mama.

Drill Sergeant: *Your favorite color is purple right*?

Me: *Yeah, it is. Why?*

Drill Sergeant: *Don't question me little girl. Are y'all done rehearsing?*

Me: *Well, you just randomly asking me my favorite color like it wasn't gonna make me suspicious. Yeah, we're finished and headed to Rissa's now.*

DRILL SERGEANT: *You sure do spend a lot of time over there. Y'all better not be sneaking no boys in while her parents are gone.*

I immediately fell out laughing at her response. It was

funny because if she only knew what had been going on at our house as soon as she and Paichence left for work and school.

Me: *Mama chill out ain't nobody sneaking in no boys over here.*

Drill Sergeant: *Yeah, whatever be home by three.*

Me: *Ok.*

"Guess the baby will be partying with us." She finally responded to my question with a giggle. "So friend, do you think I should tell my parents I'm pregnant before or after graduation?"

"It depends. Have you been to the doctor aside from the trip to the emergency room?"

"No, I actually have an appointment on Friday."

"I say wait until after your appointment. That way you can answer any questions they might have."

"Yeah, that makes sense. I'll just wait til then to tell Brandon's ass too." She said rolling her eyes.

"What you think he's gonna say?"

"Ain't no telling." She started before the ringing of her phone interrupted her. "Can you grab my phone outta my purse and see who it is?"

"It's your Slugga Boooo." I teased passing her the phone so she could answer it.

Not wanting to be in their conversation, I pulled out my own phone to text my man even though he probably can't respond right now.

Me: *Hey baby just hitting you up to let you know I'm thinking about you. Love you.*

My Love: *Sup lil mama? A nigga miss you too, especially this morning. What you got up?*

Me: *Just leaving rehearsal and riding with Rissa. What about you?*

My Love: *Stopped for a lil break to get something to eat. Bout to get back on the road so I can finish early enough to see you hit that stage this evening.*

Me: *Well on that note don't let me hold you up. Talk to you later.*

"Friend I'm about to go meet up with Slugga you riding?"

"Nah, I ain't tryna be no third wheel. You can take me home and I can get me a nap in." I told her as I tried to stifle a yawn.

"You sleep more than me and I'm the pregnant one." She said side eyeing me.

"Unt! Unt! Don't be looking at me like that slut, you are the pregnant one." I told her while inwardly praying that nothing came of the wild weekend Lynx, and I had in Biloxi.

Five minutes later we were pulling into my empty driveway which meant my mama was probably still at the hair salon. It was a little before noon and I was about to take a relaxing bubble bath before taking a nap.

"Aight friend I'll see you later." I told Rissa as I made sure I had all of my things before getting out of the car.

"See you later my fellow graduate." She replied in the corniest voice ever and we both fell out laughing.

Once I unlocked the door, I waved to Rissa before going in and locking up behind me. I grabbed a bottle of water from the kitchen and went in the bathroom to start running my bath water, adding some bubble bath. While the water was running, I went into my bedroom to get something comfortable to sleep in. I turned the radio on and popped in an R&B mixed CD I made the other day using LimeWire and it had all the hot shit on it. I turned the radio up loud enough to hear it while in the bathroom, grabbed everything I needed, and went back to the bathroom. Turning the water off, I peeled off my clothes, put my shower cap on, and submerged my body in the hot water. My body instantly felt relaxed as I giggled thinking about Lynx saying, I bathed in water hot enough to boil crabs.

After soaking for about twenty minutes and adding in more hot water, I finally washed up twice, rinsed under the shower and got out. I finished handling my hygiene and slipped on my t-shirt and shorts, after thoroughly moisturizing my skin. Sliding my feet into my slippers, I put my clothes into the correct hampers and went to my room and tied my scarf around my wrap cap. I grabbed the remote turning the volume down on my radio before turning it completely off, I set my alarm, climbed into bed, pulled the covers over my head and before I knew it, I was out like a light.

BEEP! BEEP! EUPHORIA! BEEP! BEEP! EUPHORIA GET YOUR ASS UP! BEEP! BEEP!

The sounds of both my alarm wailing and my mama screaming jarred me from the good ass sleep I was getting as well as interrupting me dreaming about riding Lynx on the interstate while he was driving. That was some freaky, kinky, dangerous shit, but I was enjoying it. I might have to run it by him to see if he wanna make that dream a reality, I thought as I got up so I could start getting myself together for graduation. I went in the bathroom to relieve my bladder and washed up, before plugging in my flat iron just in case I needed to touch up my hair.

The growling of my stomach sent me straight into the kitchen where my mama was sitting at the bar on the phone running her mouth. I went into the fridge to grab everything I needed to make me a sandwich. I popped the bacon slices in the microwave and lightly toasted the bread before spreading a layer of the mayo and mustard I had mixed together on it. Next, I added some shredded lettuce, tomato, and pickle slices before adding my turkey, ham, bacon, and cheese. Once I had my sandwich assembled, I cut it in half, poured a little plain Lay's on the plate, and grabbed a Sprite out the fridge before taking it over to the dining room table. I was starving so I quickly blessed my food and dug in.

I finished eating and checked the time, I needed to get a move on it so I wouldn't be late. Going into the bathroom, I brushed my teeth first before I started my hair. I removed the scarf and wrap cap and began combing my hair down. My hair had really grown, even with the trim Torsor gave me yesterday it still had a lot of length. Once I had it combed out and I had my middle part perfected, I passed the flat iron through a few pieces that had puffed up a little at the roots before going back in my room. My black dress was hanging on the back of the door along with my gown, so it didn't get wrinkled. I pulled the box with my shoes out of the closet and sat it on the floor next to my bed before going over to my dresser and pulling out a red matching bra and panty set.

Once I was dressed, I stood looking at myself in the mirror. The sleeveless black pinstripe dress contoured to my body perfectly and clung to my hips stopping just above my knees. Instead of my signature monogram earrings and name-plate chain, I opted for my diamond studs, matching pendant necklace, plus the key necklace from Luxe, and my charm bracelet. Stepping into the black, stiletto sandals, I fastened the straps and secured the graduation cap on my head and made sure not a hair was out of place. Then I went into the living room where some of my family members were gathered, we took a bunch of pictures before it was time to go. I went back to my room and spritzed myself with some Curve perfume before grabbing my purse, phone, and gown. Everyone shuffled out of the house and to their respective vehicles. I handed Paichence my gown so she could hang it on the hook in the back and I climbed in the front passenger seat of my mom's Navigator. I pulled out my phone and saw I had text from Lynx, hoping he wasn't telling me he was gonna miss my graduation I quickly opened it.

My Love: *Hey Lil Mama just letting you know I'm headed home to get ready, and I'll see you later on tonight, love you.*

Me: *I can't wait to see you later, love you too.*

Once we made it to the church, she let me out and I grabbed my gown and went inside to find Rissa.

SPECIAL DAY

Special Day
Lynx Malveaux

I worked my ass off to finish my route early enough to make it home, shower, get dressed and make it to the church on time. A nigga was genuinely excited for lil mama and her achievements. She and Rissa both are graduating with honors and in the top ten of their class. I already knew they were smarter than a muthafucka but this shit here only confirms it. My lil mama has been kind of sad since it's another milestone in her life her dad would be missing. I just hope the surprise I have for her will cheer her up, I thought as I pulled into my driveway and the smile quickly disappeared from my face. What the fuck is she doing home I wondered as I parked behind Miranda's truck and pulled out a pre-rolled joint sparking it up.

It's a damn shame a man gotta get high before going inside his own fucking house. I tell you what, I'm definitely not in the mood for her bullshit. Today I'm on whatever the fuck she on, so she better tread lightly, I thought as I continued smoking my joint listening to the radio. Once I had finished my joint, I sprayed my truck and waited for it to air out before going inside. Miranda was in the kitchen cooking, and I spoke hoping she didn't start the stupid shit. She spoke back dryly, *"here we go with the dumb shit,"* I thought inwardly.

"What you cooking?" I asked because I thought I smelled tomato sauce.

"Lasagna." Yeah, she is most definitely on the stupid shit but I'm gonna show her ass two can play the stupid game.

I walked down the hall to check in on the kids. LuLu was in her bed sleeping so I gently kissed her on her forehead and eased back out of her room. LJ was in his room playing the game.

"Sup son? You finished your homework?"

"Yes sir." He responded without looking away from the TV.

"Aight, I'll check you out later." I told him and closed his door before going into our bedroom. I went straight to our bathroom, took a leak, stripped down tossing my uniform in the dirty pile with the rest of them, handled my hygiene and then hopped in the shower. I washed up twice before rinsing and getting out and wrapping the towel around my waist. I put my deodorant on, went back in the room and headed straight for the closet. I grabbed my overnight bag that was already packed and the clothes I had already picked to wear for the night. After getting dressed in a pair of black, casual Polo pants, a black Polo shirt with the white horseman, and finished my look with the white and black Jordan 12 Low Taxis that came out last week.

Once I was dressed and satisfied with my appearance, I sprayed myself with some of my Issey Miyake cologne and tossed it in my bag. I double-checked making sure I had everything I needed and grabbed my bag, keys, and wallet. Checking the time, I was right on schedule. I stopped by LJ's room again to tell him I was out, but he had fallen asleep as well. I took a deep breath as I proceeded to the dining room to leave because I didn't know how this shit was gonna play out with Miranda but deep down, I really didn't care.

"Dinner's almost-" she started and stopped once she noticed the bag on my shoulder and her eyes turned to slits. "Where are you going all decked out and with an overnight bag?"

"The fuck away from here." I told her not really interested in the conversation.

"You look like you don't plan on coming home tonight."

"That's cause I'm not."

"And why the hell not?" She asked as her voice rose several octaves. I know damn well this muthafucka ain't getting loud with me.

"Didn't you tell me when I first got home you was cooking lasagna?"

"Yeah, and what's wrong with that?"

"If you can't figure out what's wrong with that picture then you have bigger problems than why I'm not coming home tonight. Later, I'm out." I told her shaking my head at her with disgust as I walked out slamming the door behind me momentarily forgetting the kids were sleep. I jumped in my truck, tossing my bag in the back. After putting my sunglasses on, I cranked up, and headed straight to Bethany Church.

Once I made it to the church and found a decent parking spot I hopped out and made my way inside. I found a seat towards the back and blended in with the crowd not really caring if anyone saw me or not. I made sure to my put phone on vibrate and began to people watch while waiting for the ceremony to start.

Some people just didn't care how they came out in public, I thought shaking my head. There was a lady a few rows up taking a seat with some see through tights on and a crop top. From what I could see her hair was way too short and thin for what was supposed to be finger waves them shits looked like fingerprints.

After almost two hours they had finally started calling the graduates and I had my camera ready to capture my lil mama. She lucky I love her ass cause graduations be long as fuck.

"Euphoria Ka'Shay Guidry." I hopped up screaming and snapping pics as she sauntered across the stage. I couldn't help but zoom in on her ass as she walked back to her seat. A nigga started mentally counting down til I have her ass folded up like some origami. She definitely had a lot of supporters shit they damn near took up a whole side. I noticed they all stood and cheered for Rissa when her name was called and assumed it was a combination of both of their families.

Once it appeared graduation was coming to an end, I pulled out my phone ignoring the multiple calls and texts from Miranda and went to me and Juvie's text thread.

Me: *Congratulations Lil Mama, you did it! A nigga so fuckin' proud of you. Go ahead and enjoy ya self with ya people and hit me up when you ready for me to come scoop you. Love you!*

I knew it would be a minute before she would be able to check her phone and see my message, but she'll respond when she does. As soon as it was over everybody started filing out of the sanctuary and heading out to find their graduate. I wanted to go find her but at the same time didn't wanna risk running into her people, especially knowing her stance on that. So, I made my way to the exit closest to where I parked and went straight to my truck. I knew it would be a few hours before we linked up, so I called mama to see if she cooked and after hearing her menu, I let her know I was on my way.

It took me a while to fight through the crowds of the church parking lot before I could get back to Plank Road. Twenty minutes later I had finally pulled up to mama's house, killing the engine I was just about to hop out when my phone rang seeing it was Miranda, I sighed before answering it. I let her know if it wasn't about my kids not to call or text me anymore tonight and ended the call. Mama was unlocking the door just as I walked up.

"Hey son, where you just coming from looking all sharp?" She greeted me pulling me in for a hug as soon as I walked through the door.

"Hey mama, Juvie's graduation."

"And you didn't tell me. How was it?"

"It was cool her and her homegirl racked up on scholarships."

"That's my girl. Where is she?"

"She's with her people, I'm gonna go get her later on."

"Y'all must not be planning on staying out too late considering it's a weeknight."

"I'm not even going home tonight."

"WHAT!" Mama screamed in shock.

"Yeah, me and Miranda got into it earlier so that just made my decision easier."

"Y'all still having issues huh?"

"Yep, and guess what she cooked today?"

"Oh Lord, I'm scared to even try to guess, just tell me."

"Lasagna."

"I'm starting to think she is doing that shit on purpose."

"You and me both."

"Well maybe a night apart would do y'all some good.

Gone in there and wash your hands and come to the table I'm about to fix your plate."

"You don't have to tell me twice." I told her before taking the short walk down the hall and to the bathroom. After pissing and washing my hands I went back to the dining room taking a seat just as mama sat the plate in front of me. The smothered turkey wings over rice and buttered whole corn was just what a nigga needed.

I hung around and chopped it up with moms for a minute before I had to go downtown to let my cousin decorate the suite I had booked for the night. I gave her a hefty tip before she left cause she did a damn good job on it. It was a little after eight when Juvie called and let me know she was ready to link up, but she told me I didn't have to come scoop her up cause her mama had finally got her a whip. She was so excited and told me she would call me once she made it so I could come down and check it out.

Forty-five minutes later Juvie was calling to let me know she had arrived, and I told her to stay in the car until I made it down. I left out of our room and took the short trek over to the elevators going down to the second floor where she was waiting for me. I called her as soon as I stepped off the elevator so she could tell me exactly where she was parked. Once I had made it over to her custom purple 2004 Nissan Maxima, she quickly hopped out and I picked her up spinning her around.

"Congratulations again love."

"Thank you, baby." She replied, leaning in for a kiss and I quickly obliged.

"Ya moms went all out on the wheels I see." I told her as I walked around checking out her ride, that was fully loaded and sitting on some chrome eighteen-inch rims. "Take a nigga for a spin." I told her hopping in on the passenger side.

"Let's go baby!" She screamed in excitement and smiling brightly.

"You hungry or need anything?"

"No, I'm stuffed we went to Don's Seafood and Steakhouse and ate since Ralph & Kaccoos had a long wait."

"That's good, I went by moms after the ceremony and ate."

"I gotta go see my girl." She said as we hit a few corners before going back to the hotel. After finding a parking spot near where I was parked, I grabbed her bag out the back before latching on to her hand leading her up to our floor.

I had Jahiem's *Special Day* playing on repeat and it had just started over as soon as we stepped into the room.

"OH MY GOD!" Juvie screamed when she saw the decorations. There were huge balloons that spelled out Congratulations and the numbers two thousand four. There was a trail of rose petals that led the way to the bedroom where a teddy bear, 4 dozen red roses and gift bags sat on the bed for her. "Baby you always show out for me." She walked over to me hugging me and planting a big juicy kiss on my lips.

"I'm supposed to and besides, I'm really proud of you. It's not too many out the hood accomplishing what you and Rissa did today. Y'all both got full rides to college, that's a blessing lil mama."

"Yeah, we really worked our asses off. I just wish my dad was here to witness it."

"I know lil mama but I'm sure he's more than proud of you."

"I got something for you." She announced changing the direction of the conversation.

"For me? What you got for me?" I asked curiously. She went in her purse and pulled out a stack of money. "What's this for?"

"My mama actually gave me back the money she made me save before she got me a car. She told me it was just to teach me responsibility."

"I'm not taking that back." I told her sternly.

"Well, what am I supposed to do with it?"

"I appreciate you for keeping it real with a nigga but I ain't no Indian giver, that's yours lil mama put it in the bank or something." I told her and she nodded. "What you wanna get into?"

"Can I shower first and then we can relax in the hot tub with some drinks?"

"Only if I can join you in the shower?" I told her biting my lip, the way the dress was clinging to her body had my dick at attention and I needed to feel her expeditiously.

"That's even better since I didn't get my fix this morning." She responded with a wink as she led the way to the bathroom.

"Wait you don't wanna open your gifts first?" I asked once we had made it to the bathroom where she started the shower.

"Nah, the only gift I'm interested in is the one standing in front of me. I'll open the others in the morning." I nodded and took off my shoes and socks before leaning against the sink.

"It's your world love. So, you gonna unwrap your gift or what?"

"Yeah, I definitely can handle that." She assured me as she sauntered over to me and started off by removing my shirt and planting a juicy kiss on my lips before tossing my shirt aside. Next, she dropped down in a squatting position unbuckling my belt and pulling my pants down followed by my boxers and I stepped out of them. My dick jumped against her lips as she kissed and licked the tip.

"Unt! Unt! Tonight, is all about you lil mama." I let her know as I grabbed her hand gently pulling her to her feet and walked her over to the awaiting shower.

Juvie stepped in first not even caring that her hair got wet. She stood her cat eye ass under the shower head as the water cascaded down her body causing my dick to get harder than Chinese arithmetic. My shit was so hard it was throbbing, I had to stroke it a little to ease the pressure. She was touching herself as we stared into each other's eyes. Not able to contain myself any longer, I scooped her up and flipped her upside down and dove headfirst into her sweetness. Of course, Juvie being Juvie, she grabbed hold of my legs and swallowed me whole. This was the most erotic sixty-nine I had ever experienced in my life and as bad as I wanted to tell her to stop, since tonight was about her, I couldn't.

Considering the position we were in, coupled with the slipperiness of the shower, I flipped her back right side up once she came in my mouth and I lapped up her juices. I didn't wanna keep her upside down too long and cause the blood to rush to her head. It took a second to get my dick out of her mouth since she was suctioning me like a Hoover three thousand but once I had her back upright, I slid her right onto my dick.

"Oooooooooohhhhhh." I slowly started to bounce her up and down while trying to keep a steady balance. I had to back myself into the corner of the shower wall when she got to bucking on my shit to prevent us from falling.

"Fuck Juvie!" I growled thrusting upward and watching my dick slide in out of her coated with her juices. Shaking my head, I had to look away before I bust prematurely. "Go ahead and cum for me lil mama." I encouraged so I could do the same. A nigga needed to get the first one off for what I got planned tonight. Ain't no sleep tonight, I'm tryna to lay in the pussy all night.

"Lynxxxxxx! Baby I'm cumming!" She screamed out and that was all I needed to hear. A few more strokes and I pulled out shooting my kids on the floor of the shower watching them disappear down the drain. We quickly washed up twice before rinsing and getting out. After quickly drying off we went back to the bedroom to get started on round two.

BABY MAMA

NARISSA TAYLOR

Taking E's advice, it was time I finally told my parents I was pregnant and Brandon too. It was the Saturday after graduation, and I had a doctor's appointment yesterday. We were downstairs having breakfast and I had already put it in my head and bucked myself up to get it over with.

"I need to tell y'all something." I blurted out after I had finished chewing my waffle.

"What's up baby girl?" My dad questioned putting his fork down giving me his undivided attention.

"Is everything ok Rissa?" My mom asked with sincerity. I took a deep breath as the tears welled up in my eyes because I knew I was about to break their hearts with my news.

"I'm pregnant." I barely whispered.

"Come again?" My dad asked as he pretended to dig in his ear like he was it cleaning out and misunderstood what I'd said.

"I'm pregnant." I blurted out a little louder this time to ensure they heard me correctly.

"Run me my money!" My mama told my daddy, and she hopped out of her seat coming over to hug me.

"Huh?" I scrunched up my face in confusion.

"I told your daddy you was pregnant, and he didn't believe me. So, we made a bet that you would tell us after your graduation and of course I won."

"So, wait how did you know I was pregnant?"

"A mother knows her child. Plus, I'd been dreaming about fish."

"So, y'all aren't upset?"

"No, a little disappointed but you're grown and as long as you're still going to college you have our support."

"Whew and I thought y'all were gonna kick me out." I let out with a nervous laugh.

"Why would we do that? You're our only child who just graduated from high school with honors and we're proud of you no matter what." My dad assured me as he got up and kissed me on my forehead. "So, is Brandon stepping up to help you out?"

"Uh, we broke up and I haven't told him yet." I cringed at the thought of having that conversation later.

"Oh wow when did that happen?" My mom asked with a face filled with concern.

"It's been a few months now."

"Are you ok? Is it permanent or do you think y'all will get back together especially with the baby on the way?" My dad asked.

"Honestly, I'm good and it is very permanent. Hopefully, we'll be able to successfully coparent. Besides, I'm seeing someone else."

"You're just full of surprises aren't you." My mom let out with a giggle. "Just know you have our full support no matter what." I smiled and nodded. If I'd known they'd be this supportive I would have been told them.

"Have you been to the doctor?" My dad questioned.

"I have and I actually had an appointment yesterday morning. I'll get the ultrasound pictures for you after I finish eating."

My parents and I continued talking as we finished up breakfast and I felt as if half of the weight have been lifted from my shoulders. I really hoped things would be this smooth when I go talk to Brandon later, but I got a nagging feeling in my gut that it won't be. Once we were done with breakfast, I helped my mom clean the kitchen before going upstairs to grab the ultrasound pics. My heart swelled with love as I watched them gush over my little red bean in the images and knew they would be excellent grandparents.

I left them downstairs before going up to shower and get dressed for the day. After getting dressed in a baby tee, some denim shorts, and a pair of gladiator sandals, I pulled my hair back in a low ponytail and swirled my baby hair. I coated my lips with my strawberry lip gloss, spritzed myself with a little Love Spell body mist, grabbed my purse, phone, keys and went back downstairs. Stopping in the kitchen to retrieve the ultrasound pictures and letting my parents know I was on my way to Brandon's house to tell him about the baby.

As I sat behind the wheel of my car messing with the radio, I ignored the uneasy feeling nagging in the pit of my stomach. Before pulling off I sent a text to E and one to Slugga with specific instructions just in case my gut was right and something bad was about to happen. It took me all of ten minutes to get to his house. I sat in the car as that uneasy feeling got more intense and took several deep breaths before grabbing my purse and pushing it under my seat. I grabbed my phone and the pictures getting out of the car and locking the doors behind me. I folded the pictures up and eased them in my back pocket along with my phone and rang the doorbell.

I knew Brandon was home because his car was out front plus I could hear the loud sounds of Boosie and Webbie's *Give Me That* blasting behind the door. I rang the doorbell for what felt like an eternity before he finally snatched the door open wearing a scowl on his face.

"The fuck you out here laying on a nigga doorbell for Rissa?" He questioned through gritted teeth which for some reason caused every hair on my neck to stand up.

"I-uh. Um, I need to talk to you, can I come in?" I asked stammering over my words.

"Nah you can't come in. Say what the fuck you need to say and step."

"Really, Brandon that's how you treat the mother of your child?"

"The fuck you just say to me?"

"I'm pregnant Brandon." I murmured.

"I know you ain't come over here to pin the next nigga's baby on me."

"Brandon, are you freaking serious right now? You're the only person I been with, which is interesting because you strapped up every time?"

"A nigga was putting holes in them shits and taking them off but seeing as how you easily hopped on the next niggas dick so fast, I'm pretty sure that baby ain't mine. Get the fuck off my doorstep and go find your real baby daddy bitch."

"You can't be serious right now. We're having a fucking baby together and like it or not we need to figure this co-parenting shit out." I yelled out in frustration.

"Rissa fuck you and that baby get the fuck outta here hoe." He yelled in my face causing spit to land on my lip and as a reflex I hauled off and slapped the shit out of him. The look in his eyes was one I had never seen before, and my instincts told me to run. Apparently, my feet and brain weren't communicating with each other because the next thing I knew he had gut punched the wind out of me causing me to stumble backwards and fall. As big as he was, he sat on me putting all of his weight on me he was punching me like a fucking nigga. My only thoughts were to protect my baby as best as I could by trying to block my stomach from his assault until he finally stopped. I laid in the grass crying, shaking, and screaming for help when I saw his huge ass foot hovering over me. I tried to quickly turn over on my side to prevent the kick from landing in my stomach but was too slow and the next thing I felt was a warm gush between my legs before everything went black.

"Hey she's awake?" I heard E say as I struggled to open my eyes trying to focus on my surroundings which were extremely blurry. The next voices I heard were my parents' and then Slugga's. Where in the hell am I and why is Slugga here along with my parents and E, I wondered. Then as if I pressed play on a movie, my thoughts replayed my last moments which led me to believe I was in the hospital and I could feel the warm tears sliding down my cheeks as I frantically began to yell, "Is my baby okay? How is my baby?"

"Rissa calm down honey or they're gonna have to sedate you." My mom spoke softly while gently rubbing my hands in a circular motion. I could tell by the tone and shakiness in her voice that something was wrong, and I started to panic. The fact that no one answered my question set off all kinds of alarms in my head and I just knew something was wrong. Before I knew it, I was crying and sobbing uncontrollably as everyone tried to get me to calm down. The doctor came in and started talking but it was going in one ear at out the other as I zoned out crying. The doctor said something to my family before injecting something into my IV and the next thing I knew I was out like a light.

I woke up to Slugga sitting in the chair next to me while holding my hand. Taking in his appearance I noticed the bandage wrapped around his hand and the dried-up blood from his knuckles that had seeped through. His unkempt braids and disheveled clothes didn't go unnoticed either. Surveying the room, I noticed all of the balloons, cards, flowers, and teddy bears which made me wonder how long I had been in this place. I gently squeezed Slugga's hand to alert him that I was up since I couldn't speak there was a tube down my throat.

"Shawty you up?" Slugga asked wiping the sleep from his eyes. He stood and kissed me on the forehead. "I'll be right back." He ran out of the room, and I assumed he was going to get the doctor or something.

"Miss Guidry, I am Dr. Spate. You've been in a medically induced coma for the past four days. You had internal bleeding, a few bruised ribs, a little bleeding on the brain which we were able to stop, and I regret to inform you that you suffered a miscarriage. I am truly sorry for your loss." Dr. Spate stated and I just stared at him with tears running down my face. "I am going to remove to the tube so you can ask any questions that you may have, ok?" I nodded my head as the tears continued to spill down my cheeks.

"Here you go Shawty?" Slugga stated after adjusting the bed so I was sitting up and placing the cup of water to my lips so I could drink. After downing the cup in its entirety and rubbing my neck. I advised the doctor I didn't have any questions other than when I could go home.

"I would like to monitor you overnight for observation. If everything checks out in the morning you can be discharged tomorrow afternoon." Dr. Spate stated before advising he would check on me later and not to hesitate to reach out if I needed anything.

"What happened to your hand?" I dropped my first question once Slugga and I was alone again.

"Let's just say I handled that nigga as best as I could before the laws could snatch him up."

"Oh boo I don't need you getting in no trouble on account of me. Where are my parents?"

"Like I said it's been handled. I just texted them to let them know you were up. They were already on their way back up here. I told them to go home to get some rest last night and I would keep them updated as well as E."

"Oh wow, this isn't how I envisioned you meeting my parents. Where's E?"

"I'm a firm believer that everything happens for a reason, but your folks cool. As for E she's been here every day as well and will be back when she gets off work." I nodded feeling a headache coming on. "What's wrong?" He must've noticed the discomfort on my face.

"My head is starting to hurt and I'm hungry."

"I'll page the nurse." Slugga let out as he laid the bed back a little for me in an effort to ease my pain.

The nurse came in and let me know what I could eat and showed me how to order it before giving me some pain meds and making sure I was good before leaving out. Slugga and I sat idly chatting until my parents arrived.

AND I

EUPHORIA GUIDRY

It had been a week since graduation, Rissa's attack, and our graduation party. Our parents thought it'd be a good idea to combine our parties and have it at the Baker Municipal Building. No expense was spared yet it wasn't the same without my best friend by my side. I tried so hard to put on a smile and enjoy myself, but it was difficult knowing Rissa was laid up in a hospital bed hooked up to machines and shit. I hated Brandon for what he did to her and I'm glad Slugga tore into his ass before the cops locked him up. I just didn't understand how he left my friend battered, bruised, and unconsciously lying in a pool of blood, I thought as I tried to shake the images from my mind while I got ready for work.

I had my shift switched to mornings since I was out of school which actually freed up my nights and weekends more. After I was dressed, I spritzed myself with some Pure

Seduction, grabbed my purse, phone, and keys before leaving out of my room. It still hasn't registered that I finally have a car and its brand new, but it feels good to not have to depend on others for a ride. I already had my license after completing Driver's Ed right after my sixteenth birthday, so I was more than ready. Of course, Miss Responsibility Teacher is making me pay my own insurance even though she added me to her policy. My phone rang just as I was walking out the door to get in my car. Seeing it was Lynx, I hurriedly answered it holding it steady between my ear and my shoulder while I locked the door.

"Hey baby, what's up?" I answered as upbeat as I could possibly be.

"Nothing much getting ready to head to work, what's up lil mama?"

"Doing the same." I let him know as I sat comfortably behind the wheel and started my car up.

"I know, I just wanted to hear your voice before I got my day started and to check on you. How's Rissa?"

"She's still in the coma as far as the last update I got before I went to bed last night but I am going up there as soon as I get off work. Thanks for checking up on me."

"You know I gotta make sure you're good. Well drive safe and I'll hit you up later."

"You too and ok. Love you."

"Love you too lil mama." He replied before ending the call and I put the car in reverse and backed out of my driveway.

It took me about ten minutes to get to work and I had to say a quick prayer before getting out when I saw Lorraine's car in the parking lot. I was not in the mood for her shit, and she can fuck around and get an ass whooping that ain't even meant for her today. I checked my appearance in the mirror and applied some more lip gloss before hopping out, locking up, and going inside to knock this shift out.

Work hasn't been the same without my best friend and I found myself having a moment in drive-thru. I quickly got myself together not wanting to have everyone crowding around me with the phony "it's gonna be okay" and bullshit that people tend to spew when people are dealing with tragedies. I was relieved when four o'clock came and I couldn't count my register down, clock out, and get the fuck outta there fast enough. I went home showered, changed, and headed straight to the hospital.

I hit the interstate and drove straight to Baton Rouge General Mid-City, the hospital where Rissa was. It took me a good twenty minutes to get there, and I lucked up on a close parking spot as someone was leaving out. Once I parked, got out, and locked my car, I went inside got a visitor's badge and took the elevator up to her floor. Taking my phone out, I noticed I had a text message from Slugga and after reading it the elevator couldn't get me upstairs fast enough. As soon as the door opened, I sprinted out of the elevator like a track star to Rissa's room.

"BEST FRIEND!" I screamed as soon as I walked in and saw her sitting up in bed.

"BESTIE!" She yelled back in what came out as a hoarse whisper, most likely due to having the tube down her throat.

"I'm so glad you're awake." I hugged her gently not wanting to squeeze to tight and hurting her. "Hey everybody!" I spoke to Slugga and Rissa's parents after showering my friend with love, and they all spoke back.

Lynx had called while I was at the hospital and wanted me to swing by Ms. Veronica's house before I went home. I stayed until visiting hours were over and Slugga walked me out since it was dark making sure I got to my car safely. Once inside, I sent a text to Lynx letting him know I was on my way and drove straight to his mom's house. I just needed to feel his warm embrace and assurance that everything is gonna be just fine.

Thirty minutes later I was pulling into Ms. Veronica's

driveway and parking right behind his truck noticing her car was missing. I got out to ring the doorbell and the door opened before I could even press the button. Looking up into Lynx's eyes as they pierced mine, I didn't even have to say a word.

"Sup Lil Mama?" He greeted me pulling me into a tight hug and kissing me on the forehead. We stood like that for a few minutes before he walked me in the house.

"Hey baby. I needed that." I told him once we'd separated from each other.

"Where's Ms. Veronica?"

"She went out to eat with her co-workers or something. So, it's just me and you tonight," he stated as he led me down the hall to his bedroom. I peeled off my clothes laying them across the chair he kept next to the door, not wanting to get in the bed with my clothes on I kept my bra and panties on before lying next to him. He pulled me on top until I was straddling him. Staring into his eyes, I leaned in to kiss him slipping my tongue in his mouth as it danced a perfect tango with his. Beneath me I could feel his manhood come alive and lifted up to remove my panties. I needed to relieve some much-needed stress and what better way than with Lynx filling my walls.

Easing down on his stiffness, I sat in place as I adjusted to his size. "Juvie what-?" I cut his question off by kissing him with so much passion my body temperature rose. I knew what he was about to say, and in this moment, I didn't give a damn about a condom, I just needed to feel him. Our eyes connected as our bodies moved in sync while I skillfully rode him just the way he liked hit.

"Fuck Juvie!" He growled out as I planted by feet beside him and slightly bounced on his dick. That shit drove him crazy, and he loved when I did it.

"Oooohhhhh Lynx. I'm about to cum." I moaned out and he grabbed me by the waist slamming me down on his shaft as he began to thrust upward until I creamed all over his dick. I collapsed on his chest trying to catch my breath and once I had my second wind, he flipped me over so that he was now on top and pinning my legs behind my head. My lil flexible ass welcomed it as I assisted by holding them in place and he slid back into me in one swift motion. He showed no mercy as he pounded me with precision making sure to hit my spot with each stroke.

"Fuckkkkkk Lynx!" I screamed out in ecstasy. "Right there, baby. Please don't stop!" I begged as he ferociously beat my kitty and I thoroughly enjoyed that shit. I love how he knows what type of sex I need and when I need it. This man knows my body like the back of his hand and never leaves me feeling unsatisfied.

The only sounds that could be heard were my moans, his grunts, and his balls rapidly slapping my ass as he continued to beat the pussy up. I let my legs down locking them around his waist pulling him even deeper inside of me, which I don't even know how that was possible. Lynx latched onto my left breast and suckled it like a newborn breastfeeding while squeezing the right one while still knocking the bottom out of my pussy.

"Ohhhhhhh shit, Lynx what are you doing to me?" I moaned out as my eyes started rolling in my head as the biggest orgasm ripped through me forcing Lynx out of me and wetting him up. That shit was explosive and took a lot out of me. As bad as I wanted to curl up in a fetal position and go to sleep, I knew I couldn't not let him get his nut off. So, me being me I flipped over til I was in the flat doggy style position, and he entered me stroking me slowly. Once I had mustered up some energy, I managed to raise up a little arching my back slightly.

"Fuck Juvie! That pussy feel so fucking good!" He whispered in my ear as he pounded me from the back. "Fuck Juvie, I can't-" was all he managed to get out before filling me up with his warm seeds. He gently laid on my back to catch his breath but making sure not to put his weight on me.

"That was everything I needed and more." I told him breaking the silence.

"Juvie you know I just went deep sea diving with no life jacket on."

"Shit happens!" That was the only response I could offer him because my brain wasn't thinking rationally at the moment.

"You already know what I told you." He deepened his voice a little and I heard his warning loud and clear before he got up and went to the bathroom. When he returned, he cleaned me up and got back in bed cuddling up close to me. Before either one of us knew it we were sound asleep.

"Heyyyyy, y'all missed check out!" A voice called out followed by rapid knocks on the door. I woke up looking dazed and confused trying to remember where I was. Lynx lay next to me knocked out snoring. I gently shook him trying to wake him up.

"Baby, get up someone's knocking on the door. They said we missed check out," I whispered as I pulled the covers up to my neck. He finally got up and went to the door cracking it open enough to poke his head out while shielding his body behind it.

"Gotcha!" I was fully awake and recognized Ms. Veronica's voice followed by her laughter. "Hey Juvie! I know you're in there."

"Hey Ms. Veronica." I managed to get out as my face grew red from shame even though she couldn't see me. Lynx closed the door and looked over at me before he started laughing and I soon joined him. Looking at the time, I knew I needed to be getting home so I got dressed and he did the same.

"You good lil mama?" He was sitting on the chair and pulled me in between his legs, and I nodded. "How's Rissa?"

"She's up and may be coming home tomorrow. It's so hard to look at her in that state while trying to keep her from focusing on her appearance. My heart broke when she found out she lost the baby. I hate him for what he did to my friend." I broke down and Lynx pulled me in his lap rubbing my back.

"That's good she's up and I know she has a long recovery ahead of her. She's gonna definitely need to lean on you for her strength. Just be there for her as best as you could, and I'll do the same for you." See this is why I love this man he's so thoughtful and attentive to my needs.

"I love you." I told him as he gently kissed my tears away.

"I love you too lil mama."

"Well, I guess I better get up from here and head on home, so you can get some rest for work tomorrow."

"You sure you good enough to drive home?"

"Yeah, I'm good." I told him getting up off his lap I grabbed my purse and keys slipping my phone in my pocket. He opened the room door allowing me to walk out first. I peeped around looking for Ms. Veronica but she wasn't nowhere in sight, so I yelled out goodnight to her and speed walked to the front door with him hot on my trail. Once we made it outside, he opened my door and kissed me.

"Be careful and call me when you make it home."

"Will do!" I told him before starting up my car and after

exchanging a few more words and kisses I was finally on my way home. It didn't take me long to get home and when I did, I called him as promised. Once he let me know he would hit me up in the morning, I went inside to shower and got my ass in the bed.

HEAVEN

LYNX MALVEAUX

It's officially summer and the city was hotter than a muthafucka in more ways than one. Miranda was still on her bullshit and whenever I didn't wanna be bothered I'd go crash at mama's house. She just didn't know every time she pissed me off, she just made it easier for me to spend time with Juvie. I don't know what she was on, but she had been showing her black ass lately. Like the old folks say something in the milk ain't clean.

I had my ears to the streets and eyes on Slugga ever since the day he popped up at my muthafuckin' crib, and from what I've been informed that nigga solid. Plus, I heard how he beat the fuck outta ol' boy who did that shit to Rissa. That's why I was headed to his crib unannounced to talk business with the lil nigga. It's time to see if the youngin' is really bout that life. My phone rang just as I turned into his apartment complex, seeing it was Juvie, I snatched it out the cupholder.

"Sup lil mama?" I answered the phone before it rolled over to voicemail.

"Nothing much just leaving the eye doctor."

"You good or you gotta get some bifocals?" I questioned

with a laugh which ended abruptly noticing she wasn't laughing with me. "Did I say something wrong?"

"I gotta wear glasses for real, while you playing." She responded and I could imagine the neck roll that went with it.

"Why you sound like that, you know you beautiful with and without them?"

"I'm gonna look like a nerd." She replied dramatically with a sigh.

"Stop being dramatic, you know your beautiful no matter what. What you bout to go into?"

"Thank you, baby but I'm still gonna look like a nerd. I'm heading over to Rissa we're probably going to go look for an apartment."

"Well, you go ahead, I'm about to handle some business. I'll call you when I'm finish and see what time you wanna get up with a nigga later."

"Okay baby. Talk to you later, love you."

"Love you too, lil mama." I ended the call and got outta my truck securing my Glock in the back of pants, so I can go run it with this nigga Slugga.

I knocked rapidly but not too hard, I ain't want the nigga to think I was the laws and get spooked or something. After a few more knocks, I stepped to the side in case that nigga came to the door like I did when he popped up at my shit unannounced. He did just as I assumed sticking the barrel of a sawed-off shotgun out the door, which was a plus in my book, stay ready so you don't have to get ready.

"Put that shit up youngin' it's me." I spoke up and he eased his head out once he locked eyes with me, he quickly dropped the gun to his side.

"The fuck you doing here OG?" He questioned cocking his head to the side.

"I came to politick with ya on the business tip." He

nodded his head before stepping aside. "After you, my nigga." I said being the smart nigga I am. Shit won't catch me slipping letting me walk in first and knock my shit loose on some get back shit.

"Ya wanna beer OG?"

"Nah, I'm good youngin'." I told him as he took a seat across from me in his living room. "So, check it I've been having my people check you out and I like what I've been hearing. One thing I like about you is that you pretty much stay to yourself and don't fuck with a lot of niggas that's a good thing. In this business you find out fast everybody ain't ya friend, some find out real soon and some find out too late, if you get my drift." He nodded as he listened intently to what I was saying, taking it all in. I rapped with him a lil longer before handing him a throw away phone and letting him know when it rings, he better answer and then I left.

It was still early, and Juvie hadn't hit me back yet, so I went to go make a few plays, collect my bread, and get the fuck outta dodge. I never sit in the same spot too long that's how niggas get fucked up in the game. Gotta move smart when you in the streets and know all money ain't good money. The streets don't play fair and at the end of the day my goal is to always make it home to my kids and Juvie no matter what.

I was driving up Plank Road heading home, when I could have sworn, I seen Miranda's truck zoom by me. Looking at the time to make sure I wasn't tripping, seeing it was only after two in the afternoon which meant she should still be at work. My curiosity got the best of me, and I bussed a U-turn to confirm my suspicions. Of course, the truck was nowhere to be found but something in me wouldn't let the shit go. I called her cell, no answer, so I called the work phone and what do you know, them people told me she was off today.

The wheels in my head were turning as I pulled over to turn around and make my way home before I spotted her ass and did something stupid.

Once I made it home, I fired up a joint and sat in my truck big chiefing. I smoked the whole joint and rolled another and smoked that shit too. After airing out my truck, I took my ass inside and stretched out on the couch. It ain't often a nigga can take a nap in the middle of the day but as high as I am I needed to sleep this shit off. Plus, I needed to have a clear head to decide how to approach the Miranda situation. I set the alarm on my phone for four o'clock, got comfortable and went to sleep.

BEEP! BEEP!

The sound of my loud ass alarm blaring in my fucking ear woke me up. Turning the alarm off, I sat up on the couch and stretched. A nigga felt refreshed, I got up to go piss and get right before I left back out. Juvie was calling me as soon as I got in my truck, and I told her to meet me by my cousin's house in Glen Oaks and she agreed. We ended the call and I saw that Miranda hadn't called me back yet, shaking my head I pulled off and headed to my people house to wait for Juvie.

My cousin was pulling into his driveway just as I was turning on his street. I pulled in right behind him and got out to go holla at him.

"What up cuz?" My cousin Rob spoke first.

"Same shit, different day." I responded and dapped him up.

"What you got up nigga?"

"Waiting on Juvie to pull up. Is it cool for her to leave her car here?"

"You know it's cool fam. Juvie got her some wheels now and she still ain't found out where you live."

"Yeah, she got it for graduation and no she ain't figured

the shit out. She thinks I live with mama. Crazy thing is when we over there she never asks about Miranda's truck."

"Wait so she knows about Miranda?"

"Shit no."

"She's rode in the truck a few times, but she more than likely thinks it's mine too."

"Nigga yo' ass wild! What you doing later?"

"Ain't no telling, why what's up?"

"Probably gonna hit the club later."

"Just hit me up and I'll let you know." I told him just as Juvie pulled up and I walked to her car.

"Say lil mama?" I told her, sticking my head in the window. "Look, park over there and come hop in the truck with me." After she had parked in Rob's yard, I opened her door so she could get out. She grabbed her stuff and got out locking up her car. I pulled her in for a hug and we walked over to where Rob was standing.

"Sup Juvie?"

"Hey Rob, what's up?"

"Chilling."

"Well, we're bout to get outta here cuz. I'll holla at you later." I opened the door so she could get in and I went around and did the same.

"What you wanna get into lil mama?"

"I was just about to ask you where we were going."

"Fuck it lets hit the slab." I pulled outta Rob's driveway and headed to Airline Highway, so I could catch the interstate and head to the city. I had no actual plans just wanted to get out and spend a little time with her since I plan to do something with the kids tomorrow. "Did y'all find a spot?" I asked remembering she and Rissa went apartment hunting earlier.

"We've narrowed our choices down to three and we're

going to make a list comparing them before making a decision."

"That's what's up. I'm surprised y'all not trying to get the full college experience and stay in a dorm."

"Before you and Slugga came into the picture that was the plan, but we'll rather have our own place and not have to deal with the hassle of sneaking y'all in our rooms and shit."

"Well, that makes sense. Just let me know how much bread you need to get situated."

"Thanks, but I should be good." This girl so damn head-strong and always wanna do everything on her own that's that Taurus in her.

"You know my birthday coming up wanna go fishing with me?"

"Hell yeah."

"Cool just take that weekend off." I told her and she nodded.

We were holding hands as I drove across the long ass Pontchartrain Bridge when *Two Occasions* by The Deele came on and Juvie turned the radio up.

A summer love is beautiful
But it's not enough
To satisfy emotions
That are shared between us

I sang over the radio stealing glances in her direction but making sure to focus on the road.

A winter love is cozy
But I need so much more
It just intensifies my wants
To have a love that endures

Of course, Juvie being Juvie she had to join in on my solo making it a duet as we sang along together.

Cause every time I close my eyes,
I think of you
And no matter what the season is,
I still love you
With all my heart
And I wanna be with you wherever you arrrrrreee

I squeezed her hand bringing it up to my mouth and kissing the back of it. The first thing we did once we made it to New Orleans was eat, a nigga had the munchies like a muthafucka. After we walked on Bourbon and Canal and got a few drinks, I was feeling good, but Juvie was out her body. The night was still young, and she wanted to go to one of the Reggae clubs. I paid the cover charge, and once inside we went straight to the bar. I ordered a bottle of water for her and a double shot of Belvedere on the rocks for me. The smoke-filled club had a nice lil vibe with women dancing and winding everywhere you turned.

Juvie was really enjoying herself dancing and winding with the best of em. She looked so fucking good doing that shit as lil beads of perspiration glistened on her forehead. Using the napkin from the bar I wiped it off as the music changed to Beenie Man and Mya's *Girls Dem Sugar.* Juvie backed into me and wound her hips rhythmically causing my dick to get hard as a brick. She looked over her shoulder at me winking as I danced with her. A crowd had started to form around us as I made sure to keep grinding against her, careful not to expose my stiffness.

"We gotta get outta here lil mama." I whispered in her ear as she continued her assault on my manhood with her ass. I was ready to fuck and now. She nodded knowingly as we made our way through the crowd and to the exit. I grabbed her hand pulling her close to me as we made our way to where I had parked. "You wanna get a room or head back home?"

"I don't have clothes or anything so we can go back home." I pulled off and headed towards the interstate when Juvie reached over and unzipped my pants pulling my dick through the slit of my boxers. She started stroking it slowly and licked her lips as the pre-cum oozed out and she leaned over and licked the tip. It took everything in me to focus on the road without wrecking as she sucked and slurped my dick like it was an ice cream cone until I bust, and she swallowed every drop. My dick was still hard and standing tall like the Statue of Liberty when Juvie slipped out of her shorts, pulled her panties to the side, climbed in my lap, and slid on my dick while I drove. This shit was next-level freaky and dangerous as fuck. She laid her head on my shoulder so I could see the road as she rode me skillfully and slowly until we both came. After a few moments she lifted up and went back to her seat. Grabbing some wipes out of her purse, she cleaned us both up as best as she could, put her shorts back on, and went to sleep. She slept the rest of the ride back to Baton Rouge. When we arrived back to Rob's house, I made sure she was good enough to drive and followed her home making sure she got inside before taking my ass home, showering, and getting some fucking rest.

NOT GON' CRY

NARISSA TAYLOR

I still hadn't fully healed from Brandon's assault, but I refused to sit in solitude sulking. The worse part of it all was as soon as I came to terms with being a mom it was snatched away from me. Luckily, I still have my ultrasound pics. My parents were distraught and angry after being so excited about becoming grandparents. Through it all, they along with E and Slugga have been supportive and catered to my every need. My parents instantly fell in love with Slugga even though I wish they could have met on better terms. I'm still on leave from work and focusing primarily on my health. I refused to let this shit break me.

E and I had finally decided on an apartment and after we were approved, we paid the deposit and the first month's rent. The two bedroom one and a half bath town home at the Bellemont Victoria was perfect for us plus it would be an easy commute to school. We were moving in on July first and were planning to go shopping for furniture this weekend and I couldn't wait.

Slugga and I were starting to get more serious, and he revealed he had a daughter who he wanted me to meet when I was ready. He let me know that he understood if I wasn't ready right now after my own loss, but I felt that it would actually be good for me to meet her. So, he will be bringing her by when he comes to visit today. I got up and carefully went into the bathroom to handle my hygiene and shower so I could get dressed for the day. I had been temporarily staying in the guest bedroom downstairs until I was healed enough to go up and down the stairs. After my shower I got dressed in a pair of black biker shorts and a white graphic t-shirt with Aaliyah's picture on it. I slid my feet in a pair of black thong sandals displaying my perfectly pedicured feet and hot pink polish on my toes. My phone rang just as I piled my hair in a messy bun on top of my head.

"Hey youuuu." I excitedly answered the phone greeting my boo.

"Sup shawty? How ya feeling today?"

"I'm actually feeling good the pain isn't as bad as it was."

"That's good. You still want us to come by?"

"Of course, I was actually about to call and see what time you were coming."

"Well, in that case I guess we can get ready to head that way. You need me to bring you anything?"

"I can't wait. No, I'm good boo. See ya soon." I told him and tossed my phone aside once we ended the call.

My stomach was touching my back, so I went in the kitchen and made me a BLT sandwich. I fixed me a glass of fruit punch and sat at the table eating. Once I was finished, I cleaned up the little mess I made, popped me two Tylenol and went to brush my teeth again. I got settled in the den and began surfing the TV channels trying to find something to watch while I waited on Slugga and his daughter. Settling on a *Moesha* marathon, I got comfortable on the recliner and tuned in.

An hour later the doorbell rang, and I got up to answer it since I was home alone. Looking through the peephole, I saw it was Slugga and opened the door.

"Sup shawty?" He smiled with a bouquet of flowers in one hand as the other hand was occupied by the prettiest little girl ever holding a cute little bear. Slugga couldn't deny her if he tried, though she was a shade or two lighter than him, she was his twin. His daughter had big beautiful, gray eyes, and a head full of long ponytails adorned with black, white, and pink balls, barrettes, and a huge pink bow on the top ponytail to match her outfit. "This is my daughter Jahzelle and Jahzelle this is daddy's girlfriend Ms. Rissa."

"Hi Ms. Rissa." She spoke in the sweetest little voice. "This is for you." She said passing the bear to me.

"Awww thank you, I love it. It's so nice to meet you. Come on in y'all." Once they were inside. Slugga gently pulled me in a hug, kissing me on the forehead and passing me the bouquet of flowers. "I'll go put these in water. Can I get y'all anything from the kitchen?"

"Nah we good. I was wondering if you wanted to get out a bit. We can grab some crawfish, snowballs and shit and go to the park."

"You had me at get out a bit."

"Yaaayyyy! We're going to the park!" Jahzelle squealed as she jumped up and down in excitement. She was so adorable in her floral print romper that tied on her shoulders and her pink gladiator sandals.

"Just let me get my stuff and we can go." I told him and he nodded. I went to the den turning the TV off, grabbed my phone and went into the guest room to grab my purse and keys. Returning to the foyer where they were waiting, we all left out, I locked up and got in the truck. Of course, he helped me in after strapping baby girl in making sure I didn't strain or pull anything.

Slugga drove as Jahzelle and I got acquainted with one another. After telling me she was four years old and telling me her birthday, she proceeded to ask me a bunch of questions. Her personality was bubbly, and she was very inquisitive. We pulled up to LTK and we all got out and went inside. After consulting with me while we waited our turn in line, Slugga placed our order for boiled crawfish, boiled shrimp, corn, potatoes, a boiled turkey neck for me and a boiled neckbone for him. Jahzelle and I had already grabbed bottled water for everybody. We left LTK and went to the nearest snowball stand before heading to the park.

We all pigged out at the picnic table and tossed our trash before taking Jahzelle to the play area. Slugga and I made small talk as we watched her carefully climb the stairs so she could come down the slide after doing that a few times, she wanted to play on the monkey bars which Slugga helped her with. After taking turns pushing her on the swing, we were all ready to leave.

"Say shawty you wanna come over and stay with us tonight?" He asked as we walked to his truck.

"Oh no, I don't wanna intrude on your daddy daughter time."

"You do know it's not an intrusion if you're invited. It'll be like a slumber party." He stated blinding me with his smile.

"Well, if you insist, I guess so. I just need to go home, pack a bag, and set the alarm."

"Fa sho."

We finally made it to Slugga's house, and I got comfortable on the couch while he went to help Jahzelle with her bath. After she was dressed in her pajamas, she came back where I was snuggling up next to me on the couch.

"Can we watch a movie?"

"Sure, how about I go take my shower and you can pick one for us to watch when I come back."

"Yaaayyyy!" She cheered, she was so stinking cute, I thought as I got up to go shower.

Slugga was coming out of the bathroom after tossing her clothes in the hamper.

"You good?" He questioned.

"Yeah, she wants to watch a movie so I'm gonna go ahead and shower."

"Cool. I'll order some pizza and we can make it a movie night."

"Sounds good to me." I told him quickly pecking his lips before going into the bathroom.

Two movies in Jahzelle had fallen asleep and Slugga went put her in her bed. "I guess it's just me and you shawty, you wanna finish watching TV in bed?"

"Yeah, we can the couch is starting to get a little uncomfortable for me." He nodded scooping me up and carrying me to his bedroom. I popped two Tylenols drinking a couple of sips of water and we got comfortable in bed finding a comedy special to watch. Slugga pulled me closer to him so we could cuddle.

"My daughter really likes you."

"I like her too. She's so pretty and funny. I hope there won't be any issues with her mom."

"Nah you ain't gotta worry about that. My baby mama know I don't play those kinda games."

"That's good." A silence fell upon us as it seems we both got lost in our own individual thoughts disregarding the TV.

"What you over there thinking about shawty?" My mind

had drifted to my baby, but I didn't wanna tell him that and damper the mood.

"Nothing much just thinking about moving and stuff."

"I know y'all are excited. I'm happy for y'all." We finally focused on the TV and laughed our asses off. We watched a few more movies before I ended up dozing off.

The next morning, I woke up in bed alone to the smell and sound of bacon sizzling making my stomach growl. I got up and went in the bathroom to handle my hygiene before coming back in the room and making up the bed. Once I was finished, I walked to the kitchen where Slugga was standing over the stove flipping the bacon and Jahzelle was seated at the table stirring a bowl of pancake batter. I stood off to the side and smiled at the scene before me prior to making my presence known.

"Good morning!" I spoke to get their attention.

"Morning shawty, I see you're up."

"Good morning, Miss Rissa. We're cooking you breakfast."

"Awww really, thank you so much." I smiled back at a cheesing Jahzelle.

"Can I help with anything?" I asked.

"Nah shawty we're just about finished." I nodded taking a seat as I watched them until the food was ready.

We sat together and ate blueberry pancakes, eggs, and bacon washing it down with orange juice. After helping Slugga clean the kitchen, we all got dressed and got our day started. Jahzelle had asked to go to Celebration Station and after assuring him I was cool with it that's where we were going first. I tossed my Tylenol in my purse just in case I needed it. Once we were all loaded up in the truck, we were headed to have some fun.

E text me while we were riding, so we were texting each

other back and forth. She wanted to know if we could go to the furniture store on Monday instead of Saturday, since she was gonna work this weekend so she could be off for Lynx's birthday weekend. I told her that was cool because more than likely I would still be with Slugga anyway.

Jahzelle had the time of her life at Celebration Station, and I must admit Slugga and I did too. We had won so many tickets that she was able to pick from the good prizes. I suggested that I cook for them, and we headed to the grocery store to get the ingredients I needed. While shopping my phone rang displaying an unfamiliar number so I didn't answer it. By the time we made it to the truck the number had called a few times and left voicemails. I listened to the messages while Slugga was putting the bags in the back. The message instantly soured my mood and caused my chest to tighten. Slugga instantly picked up that something was wrong and questioned it.

"That was the district attorney's office calling to let me know Brandon had just been released on bond."

"Damn, I thought he didn't have one."

"I don't understand what changed." I said aloud as I trembled with fear.

"Let's just go to your house so you can grab some more of your stuff, and you can stay with me for now."

"Are you sure, I don't wanna impose?"

"I wasn't asking." Ok, this nigga taking charge, I like that I thought to myself. "I'd rather know you was safe then way across town by yourself in danger." I agreed because he was right.

LOVE YOU DOWN

EUPHORIA GUIDRY

Lynx and I had a great time for his birthday weekend ducked away. We caught plenty of fish, went to the beach, and did anything else we thought to do. Once we made it back home, I finished getting everything ready for our move. My mama was against it at first, but it wasn't like she could stop me. I'm legally grown and it's no different than me going off to college and staying in a dorm. Rissa's parents are cool with it of course, especially with Brandon out on bond.

I had been missing my dad a lot lately, so I wrote to him asking if I could finally visit and he agreed. After speaking with Lynx, he told me he'd drive me so I wouldn't have to go alone. Luckily, he is in a facility in Louisiana I didn't really know much about the FEDs, but I know sometimes people are sent out of state and shit. I haven't seen my dad in years because he wouldn't allow my mom to bring us to visit him there, so this will be very interesting.

Rissa's parents hired a cleaning company to come in and professionally clean the apartment for us, but we still went behind them and did our own additional cleaning as we waited for our furniture to be delivered. We had our closets filled with our shoes and most of our clothes. The kitchen and bathrooms were completely finished and decorated to our liking. We had the wall décor up on the walls of the living room and our bedrooms so we really wouldn't have much to do but put our bedding on the beds and other minimal stuff.

"Friend everything is coming along good." Rissa said as we stood around the living room admiring our work so far.

"Yes, it is and I'm so in love with my room."

"I can't lie friend I was worried how it would turn out when you said purple, ivory, and black but that shit is the bomb. I just knew you were gonna go overboard with the purple, but you didn't."

"I know you're not talking with all that damn pink and white. Slugga probably ain't gonna wanna come in there." I playfully teased her about her room colors since pink was her favorite color.

"Girl boom, Slugga wanna be anywhere I'm at. If he could he'd probably live in my skin."

"Okkkkk friend that's what I'm talking about and y'all still ain't have sex yet?"

"Nope but I think I'm ready."

"Have you told him yet?"

"Nah, knowing Slugga he'll make me get clearance from my doctor first."

"Rissa that man cares about you and is only concerned about your overall well-being, especially after the trauma your body experienced. Just talk to him friend and if that doesn't work just take the dick." I told her and we both busted out laughing.

"I was just gonna take it without talking to him." It felt good to have my friend back to her old self. It took her a while to get back here, and I actually thought she'd have a setback with Brandon out, but she's been doing good. There's a restraining order in place but at the end of the day that shit is just a piece of paper, so she has shit like mace, a pocketknife, her dad is taking us to the gun range and to get licensed because he said we both need a gun for protection.

The delivery guys from Royal Furniture finally arrived with our living room set, end tables, dining room table and chairs, and both of our complete bedroom sets. We covered most of the costs for our furniture and Rissa's parents covered the rest as a housewarming gift. My mom's gift consisted of an entertainment system for the living room and TVs for the living room and our bedrooms. They all came by that evening to see the apartment and make sure we were good. I was so happy when they left so Lynx could come over.

"Bitch, are you gonna ever introduce him to your family?" Rissa asked once it was just us again.

"I mean I want to, but you know how Karla is and at the same time something in the back of my mind is telling me not to."

"How long do you think that man is gonna allow you to keep him a secret?"

"To be honest, I don't even think he cares. He always says it's whatever I'm comfortable with."

"I'll tell you what, your ass is damn good at hiding the shit for almost two years."

"I know huh, I'm a pro at this shit." I high fived her as we giggled.

"Well friend I'm gonna get ready to go see my man so y'all can have some privacy."

"Unt, unt bitch, is that code for you're not staying home our first night in our apartment?"

"I'll be back later."

"Girl boom, you know that man is not letting you drive across town in the middle of the night."

"Yeah, you're right. Just tell Lynx to stay here with you so you won't be alone if you're scared."

"Whatever bitch." I told her flipping her off and sticking my tongue out at her as she got up to go upstairs to her room.

I got up and went upstairs to shower before Lynx made it and put on something comfortable.

"Friend, Lynx is downstairs and I'm leaving." Rissa called up to me.

"Ok tell him I'll be right down and call me when you make it to Slugga's."

"Bitch he can hear you and I will." I giggled when what she said registered. I was comfortable as fuck in a tank top, some lil track shorts, toe socks, and slippers as I made my way downstairs.

"Hey baby." I walked over to where Lynx was sitting on the couch and climbed in his lap kissing him.

"Sup lil mama you must've missed a nigga?"

"You know I always miss you."

"You better. Damn you smell good." He said nuzzling my neck and inhaling my scent. "Y'all got it decked out in here to say y'all just moved in this muthafucka today. You gonna give a nigga a tour?"

"Come on so I can show you around." I told him as I got up off of his lap so he could stand up.

"I'on know what you trying to pull 'em down for cause that ain't helping." He said as I was attempting to pull my shorts down that had crawled up my ass. "I know you better not where them muthafuckas outside as a matter of fact them for my eyes only." He winked smacking me on my ass as he followed behind me.

"You want something to eat or drink?' I asked him while we were in the kitchen.

"Nah, I'm good but a nigga shole is looking forward to some home cooked meals."

"You know I got you baby." I told him as we went upstairs, and I showed him around.

"Damn Juvie. This shit sexy ass fuck." He said looking around my room taking it all in.

"I knew you was gonna have the color purple somewhere in here."

"This is still one of my favorite pictures." He stated picking up the fuzzy purple picture frame off my nightstand with the picture we took in Biloxi for my birthday when he took me to that fancy restaurant.

"Yeah, mine too. We were fly as hell." He nodded putting the picture back in its place. "You wanna stay up here or go back downstairs?"

"Shit, we in the right place as hard as you got my dick, prancing around him them lil ass shorts."

"Oh, is that right?" I questioned cocking my head to the side and grabbing a handful of it. He definitely wasn't lying he was so hard my mouth began to water.

"Damn Juvie you got that look in your eyes, what you bout to do to a nigga?" I didn't even answer I just dropped down in a squatting position cause I wasn't about to subject myself to carpet burns. I unbuckled his pants freeing the beast from his boxers that thang jumped out and tapped me on the mouth. Tugging his pants down I wanted all that shit off cause I was about to deepthroat that dick just the way he liked it. Yeah, I'm glad Rissa did decide to leave I thought to myself as I planted my feet on the floor making sure I was comfortable before I started. I teased the tip of it with my tongue and it jumped. I looked up and Lynx was staring at me, and I was staring at him and in one swift motion I swallowed him whole. That nigga got weak in the knees, flinching since I hit him with the unexpected. I continued my deepthroat assault allowing his mushroom head to tickle my uvula as we continued our stare down.

"Unt! Unt! Juvie that's enough!" He moaned out as he withdrew himself from my mouth and I licked my lips and winked at him. "You better not ever do that shit to nobody else you hear me?" I nodded as I giggled and the expression on his face let me know he was serious.

"Baby you remember this?" I asked since I was still in the squatting position, I started doing the monkey on a stick dance. He didn't answer so I looked up and he was stroking his dick.

"I got the stick or should I say the dick for you to monkey on." He reached for my hand pulling me up. "You know I ain't finna let you outdo me, right?" I nodded because I knew he was about to commit a 187 on my pussy with his tongue. "Go ahead and sit up in the bed with ya back against the headboard so you can experience an assault and a stare down at the same time like you just did me." He told me while pulling his shirt over his head and tossing it to the side. I moved in slow motion because I didn't know if I should be excited or afraid.

Lynx pushed my legs up and spread them apart like he was about to give me a pap smear before he got in position. He teased my clit with his tongue as his eyes bore into mine and without warning he stuck his entire tongue in my kitty licking and slurping my sugar walls. The shit was too intense, my breathing was becoming labored, and I wanted to break our stare so bad, but the connection was so strong it was as if I was in a trance. I couldn't even moan out loud, yet I was moaning in my head. For some reason it felt as if he could hear me because every time, I moaned in my head he would fuck me with his tongue. Unable to speak, I abruptly came without announcing it. He didn't stop licking and slurping until he had gotten every drop. Once my breathing had somewhat regulated, I slid downward until my head was laying on my pillow. My eyes fluttered as I stifled a yawn.

"Ain't no sleeping lil mama, daddy brought dick too." He stated as he rolled the rubber onto his stiff dick. Climbing into the bed, he hovered over me as his mushroom head tickled my entrance. Tracing my lips with his tongue ring had long become the norm for us before slipping his tongue in my mouth. I could taste my own sweetness coupled with the traces of mint on his breath making the kiss even more pleasurable. Tonight, was all about no warnings because there was none when he entered me fully until he was balls deep. My eyes widened as he stretched me out as he continued kissing me, taking my mind off of it until I had adjusted. I rotated my hips meeting his thrusts creating our own rhythm as we moved in sync with each other. He stroked me long and deep luring another intense orgasm from my core that it caused my legs to shake.

"You ready to come monkey on this dick?" I was tired and spent but I couldn't deny my man and cause him to have blue balls. So, once he pulled out, we switched positions, and I mounted him so I could honor his request. One thing about me being on top is I controlled the show and I knew what I needed to do to make him cum quick. Lynx had worn my ass out, but I refuse to ever tap out first.

RUNNING OUT OF LIES

LYNX MALVEAUX

"FUCK!" I jumped up outta my sleep checking my watch, I see it's almost three in the morning. Now I'm scrambling to get dressed without waking Juvie up so I can get home, get dressed and make it to work for five since I agreed to go in early. It wasn't my intention to fall asleep but shit after the way we fucked, sucked, and slurped each other the only thing we could do was clean ourselves up and crash. Once I was dressed, I kissed Juvie on the forehead and whispered I love you in her ear and she didn't even flinch. My baby was tired as hell, I pulled the covers up to her neck left out of her room closing her door behind me. I quietly went down the stairs as fast as I could in case Rissa had come back, I didn't want to wake her up. I left out locking the door behind me and making my way to my truck.

As soon as I was behind the wheel, I started my truck, and waited a few minutes before pulling off and heading home. I made it there in no time since there was barely any traffic on the road. The house appeared to be still, so hopefully I could get in and get out without having to hear Miranda's mouth. I got out going inside and as soon as I stepped into the dining room, the light flipped on, and she was sitting at the table. If looks could kill, I'd be six feet under right now.

"Where the fuck have you been?" She hissed at me assuming she didn't wanna wake the kids.

"Look, my bad for just getting in but you better get your muthafuckin' mind right talking to me like you don't have no sense."

"I wanna know what bitch got you not coming home." I was about to tell her ass the truth when I remembered something.

"And you know what I wanna know?'

"What the fuck do you wanna know Lynx?"

"You got one more time to come out the side of your neck to me. So, where were you a few Fridays ago after two? Make sure you think long and hard before you answer."

"I was at work where else would I be?" She responded by rolling her eyes as she spoke.

"Is that your final answer or do you wanna phone a fucking friend?"

"Yes, it's my final answer, why wouldn't it be, when that's where I was?"

"Well, Lil Miss I was at work where would I be? I thought I saw your ass fly by me on Plank Road around that time, so I called your job after calling your phone and not getting an answer. Imagine my surprise when they told me you were off that day, but I distinctly remember you getting your ass up and dressed for work." I swear all the color drained from her milk chocolate face telling me all I needed to know, and I walked the fuck off. Glad I followed my first mind and sat on that shit instead of checking her when it happened.

I went in the bedroom and straight to our bathroom quickly handling my hygiene before hitting the shower so I could get dressed for work. When I walked out of the bathroom, Miranda was sitting on the bed looking all sad and shit. I moved around the room ignoring her ass as I hurriedly got dressed so I could make it to work on time. As soon as I was ready, I grabbed everything I needed and walked out of the room.

"So, you're just gonna ignore me?" She questioned walking behind me as I continued my stride ignoring her.

"You ready to answer my question?" She got quiet and the expression on her face let me know she wasn't, so I continued walking until I reached the dining room, opening and closing the door in her face. I hopped in my truck, started it, and hauled ass to work.

A nigga was so glad when my shift had finally ended, I was ready to go home and shower. My phone rang as soon as I got in my truck, seeing Juvie's name on the display I quickly answered it.

"Sup lil mama?" I spoke as soon as our call connected.

"Heyyyy you. Why didn't you wake me up when you left?"

"Cause it was too early in the morning and you were knocked out."

"Where'd you run off to?"

"I had to go in to work early and I needed to go home and get dressed."

"Well, I guess I can let you slide."

"What you up to lil mama?"

"Nothing much, bored, laying down watching TV."

"Where's Rissa?"

"She and her parents had to go meet with the DA about her case."

"Oh ok. What you got up later?"

"Nothing much. About to get up and cook. What about you?"

"I just got off and headed to shower before I go get LuLu from daycare. I gotta swing by mama house and run a few errands but that's about it."

"Well, go ahead and handle your business grab you some clothes and come by when you're done, we can eat and watch a movie." I was about to decline when I remembered Miranda didn't disclose her whereabouts.

"Ok lil mama, I'll hit you up when I'm on my way. Love you."

"See you then. Love you too." She replied before we ended our call.

I continued driving until I made it home and went inside doing just what I told Juvie I was about to do. After getting dressed, I grabbed my bag and everything else I needed and left. I went to get baby girl from daycare before going by mama's house since LJ was still at summer camp way on the other side of town. LuLu was excited to see me when I went in to sign her out. I strapped her in car seat and drove straight to mama's house.

When we arrived, I got her outta her seat and carried her to the door. Mama opened it before I could even ring the doorbell. "Hey MawMaw's, pretty baby." She said taking LuLu clean out my arms.

"Sup mama?" I spoke to her since LuLu had all of her attention.

"Hey son, how's everything with you?"

"Stressful as ever."

"Oh Lord, what you got going on now?"

"Miranda been moving kinda funny and when I asked her about it, she lied. I let her know I knew she was lying, and she couldn't say anything." I told her before I ran the whole situation down to her.

Once I was done telling her everything, she just looked at me and shook her head. "So basically, you're mad at Miranda because she might be doing the same thing you are doing. You know they say what's good for the goose is good for the gander?"

"Really, mama whose side are you on?"

"I'm not on anybody's side because I been told you about your shit. Weren't you supposed to be telling Juvie the truth when y'all went fishing? I'm telling you when that girl finds out it's gonna blow up in your face."

"I was gonna tell her but now that she got her own place, I figured I didn't need to. She's on one side of town and Miranda's on the other so no need to mess up a good thing."

"I swear you just like your damn daddy." She said getting up and sitting LuLu on the couch next to me before going into her bedroom and slamming the door. Yep, she's pissed with me, I thought as I sat there replaying our conversation.

After sitting there for a few minutes, I picked up LuLu and we headed out so I could run my errands. Once I was done, it was almost five in the evening, so I headed home to drop LuLu off. When I pulled up LJ was outside in the backyard throwing the football around.

"What's up son?" I called out to him when we got out of the truck.

"What's up dad?" He walked over to me dapping me up as I put LuLu down so she could run around a little.

"Nothing much wanna throw the ball a bit before I head out?"

"Yes sir." He replied tossing me the ball and running out in the yard so I could throw him a long pass. We took turns throwing the ball to each other before Miranda came outside and told him to go get cleaned up for dinner. "Dad will I be able to try out for football this year?"

"Yeah, I'm gonna talk to your mama about it again. Miranda wouldn't let him try out last year talking about he was too little, and he had a fit."

I scooped up LuLu and led the kids back into the house. She was in the kitchen cooking something. Knowing her ass it was probably some shit I was allergic to, but I didn't ask cause I was about to leave anyway. I told the kids I would see them later and left out. I sparked up a joint as soon as I got in my truck before pulling off enroute to Juvie's crib. I called her to let her know I was on my way and see if she needed anything. She said she didn't, but I stopped by the store and grabbed a bottle of Amaretto, a jar of cherries, and some pineapple juice.

Once I pulled into her complex, I parked near their building. I grabbed everything so I had to only make one trip. I knocked on the door and Juvie answered, dressed in a tank top, some really short denim shorts, and fuzzy slippers. The way that ass was sitting in them shorts instantly made my dick come alive.

"Sup lil mama?" I pecked her on the lips. "Damn it smells good, what you in here whipping up?"

"Smothered porkchops, rice, green beans with potatoes, and cornbread."

"You tryna put a nigga in a food coma." I told her sitting the bag with the drinks on the counter. "I'm gonna go put my clothes in your room, I'll be right back."

When I came back downstairs, I noticed the music playing that I didn't realize was playing at first. I got comfortable on the couch and vibed to R. Kelly while I watched her move around the kitchen. "I brought us something to sip on lil mama. You want me to fix us a drink now or after we eat?"

"What you got?"

"Amaretto and pineapple juice."

"I've never had it before, but you can fix it now."

"I'm telling you now, it's smooth as fuck and will sneak up on you, so sip it slow."

"We'll see."

"Ok smart ass, don't say I didn't warn you."

"I'm a big girl. I can handle it."

"I got something I know you can handle for sure." I told her grabbing my dick.

"And can." I maneuvered around her getting two glasses and adding ice so I could make our drinks. I poured the Amaretto in the glasses, then added the pineapple juice, and finished it with a cherry on top.

"Here taste this lil mama." I told her as I passed her one of the glasses and she took a sip.

"Damn this is good." She stated before taking even bigger sips."

"Girl, slow down." I warned her ass again, before taking my drink into the living room and sitting on the couch.

After she finished what she was doing she came and sat next to me propping her feet in my lap. We sat there and vibed out to the music and just talked about random shit while we waited for the food to finish.

"Is it cool if I smoke in here or do I need to run to my truck?"

"Hell yeah, as long as you let me hit the shit."

"Juvie, since when do you smoke?"

"I blow occasionally."

"Why you never mentioned it before?"

"The conversation never came up." She responded

hunching her shoulders. I pulled the green from my pocket and rolled up two joints.

"Never smoke nothing you didn't roll or see rolled. I don't give a damn who it is, you understand lil mama?"

"Yes, just like I know never to leave a drink unattended in the club, then go back and drink it."

"You muthafuckin' right. People are fucked up outchea and you bout to start college life, so it's only right I put you up on game." I told her as I passed her the joint and lit it for her. She pulled it hard and started coughing. "Yeah, that's that gas, nigga don't smoke no bullshit."

"I see." She managed to get out after she had stopped coughing. "Now that I know. Let me try this again." This time she hit it with no problems blowing the smoke out her nose.

"Pass that shit and go check the food before you get too fucked up and burn it."

"Never that, I'm a professional boo." She passed me the joint and got up putting all that ass in my face. I couldn't resist slapping and watching it jiggle. This silly ass girl clapped each one of her ass cheeks individually then clapped them together before walking off. I couldn't do nothing but shake my head as I inhaled the weed watching her as she washed her hands first before checking the food. "It's ready you wanna finishing smoking or eat first?"

"Let's go ahead and kill this one then we can eat." After we finished smoking, I went to the bathroom to take a leak and wash my hands while she made our plates. When I walked back to the front, she was sitting our plates on the table. "You want me to fix you another drink love."

"Yeah, I should be good. I don't have to go to work til nine."

"I'll make you a half a one cause you gonna be good and fucked up when it kicks in."

"I'm already feeling it or maybe that's the weed either way I feel something." She said as she took her seat at the table. I refilled our drinks and took a seat across from her. The plate in front of me looked like one of them plates grand-mama makes.

"Damn Juvie this ain't no gravy packs this some official cooking here."

"It sure ain't, I told you I could cook." I nodded and we said grace before digging in our food.

"Oh yeah, you can definitely cook lil mama." I stated honestly. I couldn't even find the words to describe how good the food taste. This girl is the whole damn package and mama want me to tell her I'm married. I think the fuck not and risk losing one of the best things in my life. Everything in this moment just felt perfect but I'd be lying if I said I didn't feel like there was something bad lurking in the shadows. "You decided on when you wanna take that ride up the road to see ya pops?"

"In the next week or two if you're free."

"Cool. I'll take off the week after next and we can go."

"Thank you, baby."

"No thanks needed. I got you forever." We finished eating and she cleaned the kitchen after declining my offer to help. She put Rissa's plate in the microwave after confirming she would be home later and put the rest of the food up.

"Come on let's go up to my room." She turned the radio off, grabbed my hand, and led the way upstairs.

KISSING YOU

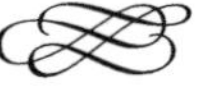

EUPHORIA GUIDRY

And I can't believe it's real
I can't believe it's you
I can't believe it's happening
I can't believe it's true
And I can't believe that you are here with me
And I am here with you (Kissing You)

I had Faith Evans *Kissing You* on repeat singing along while I cooked breakfast for Lynx and me. Rissa's ass was at Slugga's house as she is most of the time unless he was out handling business. Then her scary ass would come home cause she didn't wanna be there alone. Her daddy made us take a self-defense class and took us to the gun range weekly until we felt comfortable enough. My friend had every right to be fearful and to be honest I didn't like being here by myself either but most of the time either she or Lynx is here.

"Morning lil mama." Lynx greeted me wrapping his arms around my waist and kissing me on the cheek as I stirred the pot of grits.

"Morning baby." I'm almost done cooking, then we can eat, and get ready to get out of here. Today is the day we take that ride to Oakdale so I can see my daddy. It was only about a two-hour drive, but Lynx refused to let me go alone. He said he doesn't feel comfortable letting me go by myself especially as a new driver and that being unfamiliar territory. If I've learned nothing else when it comes to Lynx Malveaux and that's to let that man be a man. Besides, I like riding shotgun and taking road trips with him. "Here you go." I told him as I sat the plate of cheese grits, scrambled eggs, bacon, buttered toast with grape jelly in front of him and handed him a fork.

"Thank you, baby."

"You know you don't have to thank me. I'll always make sure you have a hot meal." I told him with a smile as I sat my plate on the table. "Do you want orange juice or something else?"

"Orange juice is cool." I nodded and added ice to the glasses before pouring the juice. After sitting our glasses on the table, I took a seat, quickly blessed my food, and started eating.

Through the night I feel your fire
And there's nothing but you on my mind
As you quench me of all my desires
And I'm filled with ecstasy
Oh, I can't believe it's real (can't believe it's real)
I can't believe it's true (can't believe it's true)
I can't believe that you chose me (can't believe)
When I was choosing you

I was lost in the music, swaying, with my eyes closed as I

chewed my food. When I finally opened them again to grab my glass Lynx was in my face. He leaned in kissing me on my forehead, then my lips. "I'll always choose you Juvie." He stated as he stared into my eyes instantly pulling at my heart strings. I was so caught up in the moment I couldn't even respond. "I know lil mama, I know." That's that soul tie shit, I didn't have to utter a word because he knew what I was thinking.

We finished eating and I cleaned the kitchen and wiped down before going upstairs so I could get dressed. Lynx was already in my room getting ready and I'm pretty sure I soaked my panties when I walked in the room seeing him. He was dressed in a pair of black BAPE jeans, a crisp white tee, a fitted cap, and a fresh pair of black Reebok Classics which everybody called Soulja Rees. The impure thoughts running through my head had my brain in a fog and the Kenneth Cole Black cologne he was wearing tickled my nose making me desire him more.

"Go ahead and get dressed with your hot ass." He spoke interrupting my thoughts.

"Why whatever do you mean?" I asked blinking my eyes while pretending I had no idea what he was talking about.

"I know that look when I see it, but we don't have time lil mama. When we get back, I promise I got you." He flashed his Colgate smile which now had my panties completely drenched.

"I was just admiring what I saw."

"So, you're saying if I stick my hand in your panties it won't drown."

"And on that note let me go hop in the shower really quick."

"Yeah, aight." He let out a chuckle before taking a seat at

my desk. I made my way to the bathroom to handle my business so we could hit the highway.

I got dressed in some black flare Levi jeans, a white baby tee, and some black and white Air Max. "Oh, you putting your ass lifters on today huh? Make me have to fuck one of them inmates up."

"Ass lifters?" I questioned confused as fuck.

"Your shoes Juvie for some reason they make your ass sit up even more. The muthafucka already big and noticeable but it's something about whenever you wear them damn Air Max, they just make it stand out even more."

"I never noticed."

"I'm pretty sure you haven't, it ain't like you walk behind yourself."

"Shut upppp!" I laughed as I finished getting dressed. "Why you looking at me like that?"

"I see ya tryna match a nigga and shit. No for real you look so cute with your glasses."

"Cute? I look like a damn nerd."

"I mean you do but a sexy one. You ready to hit the slab lil mama?"

"Oh whatever. Yeah, I'm ready."

We grabbed our stuff and made our way downstairs. I locked the door and followed him to his truck. He helped me in before going around getting in the driver's seat. "Find us some riding music."

"Anything particular you wanna hear?"

"I'm good with whatever you pick."

"Well since you insist." I pulled the *Waiting to Exhale* CD outta my bag and popped it in. I went straight to the song I was looking for and turned the radio up.

"Really, Juvie?" He looked at me and shook his head cause I

was playing Faith Evans *Kissing You* again. "I'mma let you vibe for now but we not listening to that for two hours." I didn't even respond because if I wanted to listen to it, he would with no problem. After playing it a few times, I switched the CD with an old school R&B mixed one. We had been riding a little over an hour and I was lost in my thoughts checking out the scenery.

"You good over there lil mama?" He asked after turning the music down.

"Yeah, baby I'm good. Why'd you ask?"

"You've been quiet for a min plus this will be the first time you seen ya pops in years, so I understand if you're nervous."

"It's weird because why should I be nervous to see my daddy like it's my first time meeting him."

"In a way it is though because it will be your first time meeting your daddy since he's been on the inside and trust me, he's a different man. Prison has the tendency to change people and not only that he'll be meeting the grown up you for the first time."

"Yeah, I guess you're right. I got so many questions I wanna ask hopefully he answers them."

"It just depends on the questions and just make sure no one can hear your conversation." He said trying to school me like I don't know the G code.

"I hear you. I wonder if he looks how I remember him."

"He may or may not especially if he be in there on them weights and shit."

"I just can't wait to see him, how much longer we got?"

"We're about thirty minutes away love." He responded then grabbed my hand clasping our fingers instantly calming me down.

"Thank you again for bringing me out here."

"What I told you about thanking me. I got you for whatever, whenever."

"It's not too many people that'll do the things you do for me and for that I'll be forever thankful. You're definitely appreciated." I leaned over kissing him on the cheek. I sat back in my seat and just enjoyed the scenery and constantly checked the clock because I was anxious to see my daddy.

We had finally arrived, and I was just taking in the scenery trying to embed everything in my memory. I wanted to remember everything about this day exactly as it occurred. Lynx's truck came to a stop when he found a parking spot.

"You ready to go in there and handle your business lil mama?"

"We're here now, it's not like I have a choice."

"You always have a choice. If you were to say you changed your mind, I'll pull off right now and head back home."

"Thanks, but I wouldn't do that. Especially since you took off work to drive me all the way out here."

"And I'd do it again in heartbeat."

"Well, it's either now or never." I inhaled, taking a deep breath, and flipped down the mirror checking my appearance. "How do I look?"

"Beautiful as always love."

"What are you gonna do while I'm in there?"

"Sit my black ass right here and wait for you."

"The whole visit?"

"Yep. Now gone on in there and see ya pops before you miss your visit."

"Ok, I'll be back soon. Thank you again for bringing me. Love you." I told him before kissing his lips.

"What I told you about that? Love you too Juvie." I got out of the truck and made my way inside.

After being searched, I was finally checked in and just waiting for them to call my name to get in line with the other visitors. Ten minutes later they called me, and I got in line. Once they had called all of the names we were led to the visiting room. My feet felt as if they weighed a ton the further, I walked into the room. I watched the other visitors as they quickly located their loved ones and embraced them.

"I'm over here Ka'Shay." It was as if time stood still when I turned in the direction of my father's voice. My feet suddenly felt like feathers as I floated over to him. "Look at you all grown up and just as beautiful as ever." He stated pulling me into his arms and I finally exhaled the breath I didn't even know I was holding. My emotions got the best of me as the tears rapidly spilled down my cheeks. This was so surreal for me right now to be in the same room literally hugging my daddy for the first time in six years.

"It's ok baby girl." He said before the CO told us to separate and sit down. "How was your drive, you didn't get lost huh?"

"Oh no, I um, um my friend actually drove me so I wouldn't come along." I stammered over my words as that question caught me off guard.

"Well, since you didn't say Rissa, I take it your friend is Lynx?" My eyes bulged out of my head, and I just know the color drained from my face, cause how the fuck did he know about Lynx.

"You know about Lynx?"

"A man of my caliber knows everything when it comes to my family and the streets. Just cause I'm on the inside doesn't mean I don't have eyes and ears out there."

"Mama doesn't know about us."

"I know and I'm not going to say anything. I will say this while I don't approve of the shit for various reasons, but I also know that you're grown and you're gonna do what you wanna do. Let that nigga know when it comes to anything that came from my nut sack, as a matter of fact, I'm gonna call you later and holler at the nigga myself. So, tell me why you were so adamant to come see me now?"

"Thanks daddy." I guess he truly has my back no matter what. "As far as Lynx, for what it's worth he treats me really good, and I really love him." I felt I needed to let him know that, but he seemed unimpressed. "I just figured you didn't want us to come visit when were younger and because I have a lot of questions that need answers, I figured now would be a good time."

"Yeah, I told your mother flat out that I never wanted you girls to see me like this, but I should have known I couldn't keep you away forever."

"So, does that mean I can visit you regularly?"

"I couldn't tell you no if I wanted to and you know that. So, let's get to these questions before we run out of time." We talked about everything under the sun, and he answered the majority of my questions. He gave me a little insight as to why my mama was so damn hard on me and even though I understood, I didn't agree with it.

The CO announced that the visit was over, and I was instantly sad all over again. We hugged each other and said I love you after he reminded me, he would be calling me later to talk to Lynx. I was so dead set on coming to visit him, that it didn't dawn on me how difficult it would be for me to leave knowing he had to stay. I cried all the way to Lynx's truck who so happened to be standing by the hood as if he was waiting on me. I walked into his awaiting arms and ugly cried.

"Go ahead and let out lil mama." He rubbed my back in a circular motion allowing me to drench his shirt with my tears.

"You good?" I nodded as my tears began to subside and I pulled away from him, drying my face with the back of my hand.

"Yeah, let's get out of here." I stated ready to get away from here. The longer we stayed here the more pain I felt knowing my father was so close, yet so far away.

"The day is still young, let's go find something fun to get into. I don't like it when you're sad beautiful." He kissed my forehead and led me to the passenger side of the truck helping me in. Once he was behind the wheel, he put the *Waiting to Exhale* CD back in skipping each track until he found what he was looking for. I smiled at him as soon as I heard the melody for Faith Evan's *Kissing You.* I knew it was his way of cheering me up since I had been playing the song all morning.

"Aren't you gonna ask me about the visit?"

"I figured you would tell me if you wanted me to know. Besides, I didn't wanna make you sad considering how you were when you came out of there."

"Well, we had a really good visit. He knows about us and is gonna call and talk to you later." I managed to get out in one breath.

"What you mean he knows about us?"

"He just said because he's on the inside doesn't mean he's unaware of what's going on in the streets."

"Juvie what's your daddy's name?"

"Ennis Guidry but everybody calls him Prime." He hit the brakes so hard, I just knew I'd have whiplash.

"Prime as in Scotlandville Prime?"

"Yeah, that's him, why you say it like that?"

"Girl, do you not know who your daddy is? That nigga is an OG and Legend in the streets of Baton Rouge." He tossed out before he started driving again.

"I guess." I told him hunching my shoulders since I don't know that side of him. "I don't know anything about his street lifestyle."

"And you won't hear it from me." Silence filled the truck as we made the two-hour drive back home.

TONIGHT IS THE NIGHT

NARISSA TAYLOR

I don't know what I did to deserve Slugga but that man is definitely heaven sent. The stress of dealing with this shit with Brandon, courts, lawyers felt like I'm being punished for his actions. Yet, through it all Slugga has been supportive and by my side. I still haven't been back to work and to be honest I don't think I want to. I've actually been thinking of finding something else or applying for work study since school starts soon. I've been joined to his hip so much I feel like a bad friend and roommate. I can count on one hand the number of nights I've stayed at our new apartment. So, I'm surprising E with a girl's night when she gets home.

"Hey bestieeee!" I sang out as soon as she answered the phone.

"Hey frienddd! What you up to?"

"Nothing much, I was just calling to see if you was coming straight home after you get off work."

"Yeah, I am. It's been a long day and it ain't even noon yet. Lorraine has worked my last fucking nerve."

"That's one thing I don't miss and one of the reasons I'm thinking about not returning."

"Yeah, I'm thinking about quitting too before I drown this bitch in one of them fryers back there."

"Friend you gonna go to jail!" I was cracking up because she would really do that shit. She's one of them people that's quiet and has a good heart but when you fuck with her, she has the tendency to snap and go too far.

"Y'all wouldn't let me sit!"

"And won't soon as you get a bond you'd be coming home."

"Fa sho. Well let me get back in here before she comes fucking with me and y'all be bonding me out for real."

"Aight friend I'll see you when you get home."

"See you then."

Since, I knew she was coming straight home, I had about six hours to run to the store and come back to get everything setup. I figured I would fry up some fish, shrimp, and fries so my first stop was to Tony's Seafood to get what I needed. We already had liquor because Slugga and Lynx always leave bottles since we're too young to buy from most places. Yet, we know where to go without having to worry about being carded when it was necessary. I would roll us up some blunts later so we could blow too.

I ran all my errands and made it back home in enough time to take a quick nap. After setting the alarm, I stripped down and climbed into my bed. Grabbing my phone, I sent a text to Slugga in case he called, and I didn't answer so he wouldn't be worried. I put my phone on the nightstand, then I rolled over and went to sleep.

An hour later my alarm was blaring letting me know it was time to get my ass up. I stretched before getting out the bed going in the bathroom to relieve my bladder and freshen up. I went back in my room to get my phone and saw I had a text message from Slugga to call him when I woke up so that's what I did. I dialed his number as I made my way downstairs to the kitchen putting the call on speakerphone.

"Sup Shawty?" He said as soon as the call connected.

"Hey bae what you up to?"

"Nothing just handling a lil business. What you up to?"

"In here getting ready to cook for me and E's girl's night." I had just finished cutting the fresh catfish filets into strips. I rinsed them and put them aside so I could peel and devein the shrimp.

"Oh yeah that's what's up. You making a nigga sleep alone tonight."

"Yeah, I been neglecting my girl and our crib, but I promise I'll sleep by you tomorrow night or you can sleep by me. Either way I have a surprise for you."

"A surprise huh? I wonder what that could be."

"I promise you're gonna love it."

"Word? Shawty, you got a nigga excited on the cool, it ain't too often I get surprises."

"Stick with the kid and you'll get surprised on the regular."

"I hear ya shawty. Check it, I'm bout to pull up to my stop and handle something. I'mma hit ya back later."

"Ok bae later." I ended the call and put my phone on the counter. I washed my hands and grabbed a paper towel going to the living room to turn the radio on. I popped in a mixed rap CD that had everything from Boosie to Soulja Slim on it. Then I went back into the kitchen to finish the shrimp. Once I had everything prepped and cleaned, I seasoned and battered everything up and waited for the oil to heat up.

I was rapping along to Max Minelli's *Nobody Move* while dropping a batch of fish into the hot grease when E walked in scaring the fuck outta me. I didn't even hear her ass come in the house.

"Bitch, you should see your face right now."

"Shut up hoe, you scared the shit outta me. Anyway SURPRISE!!!" I screamed out and she looked at me confused.

"What you mean surprise?"

"I felt bad for ditching you for Slugga all the time, so I thought I'd surprise you with a girl's night."

"Awww friend you didn't have to do that. I understand wanting to be caked up with ya man."

"I know friend, but I just wanted to do something nice for you, so I cooked. I'm gonna mix us some drinks up, and I got some weed and cigars on my dresser to roll up too."

"Oh bitch, that sounds like a plan. Let me go upstairs, to shower and change and I'll come down to roll up." I nodded and finished rapping until I had cooked everything and put it in the oven to stay warm. I grabbed an empty pitcher and rinsed it out before making some Incredible Hulk by mixing Hennessy and Hypnotiq. I put the pitcher in the freezer so it could chill and went upstairs knocking on E's door.

"Come in!" She yelled out.

"I just wanted to tell you the food is ready and in the oven on warm. The drink is in the freezer chilling, I'm about to shower, and then I'll meet you back downstairs."

"Cool, I'm just talking to Lynx and rolling up before I go back down."

"Sup bro?" I yelled loud enough so he could hear me.

"He said what's up?"

"Chillin' like a villain." I replied and fell out laughing before leaving back out of her room and going to mine.

After showering, I did my face routine and moisturized my skin before slipping on a tank top, shorts, flip flops and going back downstairs. E was in the kitchen fixing our plates and I grabbed the ketchup and hot sauce out of the cabinet putting them on the counter. I got our glasses, added ice, and poured our drinks sitting them on the table before going back to grab the condiments and silverware. She brought our plates, and we quickly said our grace so we could start eating.

"So friend how do you feel after going see your dad? I mean was it a one-time thing or do you think you wanna go on the regular."

"I wanna do it on the regular but friend I cried like a baby when I realized I had to leave him in there. Other than that, we had a good visit and talked about a lot of stuff. He even knew about me and Lynx's relationship."

"That's good but how the fuck did he know about y'all, and Mrs. Karla don't even know."

"I have no idea but when I told Lynx he asked me daddy's name and when I told him that nigga hit the brakes in the middle of the street. Something about daddy being a legend in the streets or some shit."

"Damn, it's crazy cause even after the shit we read and saw on the news I still don't believe he was guilty of any of that shit. If he did do that shit, he was excellent at hiding it cause I swear he just worked a regular nine to five." I told her popping a shrimp drenched in ketchup and hot sauce in my mouth.

"Shit, you and me both. He even called later and talked to Lynx, but he won't tell me what they talked about."

"You know he probably threatened that nigga. On some he better not break your heart, cause he'll break his legs or some shit like that."

"I hope not but enough of that topic you and Slugga got down yet?"

"No, not yet but I told him I got a surprise for him

tomorrow night. He just don't know he bout to come up off that dick."

"That's right friend, get him." She reached over high fiving me as we continued eating.

"Oh, trust me I am."

Once we finished eating, she grabbed our plates and took them to the kitchen. "I'm gonna do the dishes and clean the kitchen right quick go ahead and fire up the killa."

"I'm already on it, friend." I grabbed one of the blunts she had rolled and sparked it up. "You want another drink?"

"Hell yeah." I went in the kitchen and passed her the blunt while I refilled our glasses. Once she was done in the kitchen, we got comfortable on the couch passing the blunt back and forth as we just talked about random shit.

"Friend we're on a countdown now we have less than three weeks until school starts, are you nervous?"

"I know and yeah, a little. I mean college is a whole new ball game."

"Yeah, it is but we got this shit friend." By midnight we both were drunk and high as hell and managed to stumble upstairs to our rooms to go to bed. I just knew the hangover we were gonna wake up with in the morning was gonna be crucial as fuck.

The next morning or shall I say afternoon I woke up with the worse hangover ever in life. I managed to stumble into the bathroom to pee and handle my hygiene. Once I was finished in the bathroom I slipped on a pair of denim shorts, a halter top, and sandals. I pulled my hair back into a low ponytail before going to check on E. I knocked on her door a few times, but she didn't answer peeping my head in the room I saw she was gone. I'm surprised she wasn't still sleeping, I thought to myself. Going back in my room I grabbed my phone to call her when I noticed a text from her letting me know she was at work so, I wouldn't be worried.

I grabbed my things so I could run to the mall. I wanted to get something sexy to wear for Slugga tonight. After going to Victoria's Secret and Fredericks of Hollywood I finally found something I thought he'd like. I made it to my car and called Slugga to see what the plan was for tonight.

"Hey bae!" I greeted him as soon as he answered.

"Sup shawty?"

"Just left outta the mall about to head home. What you up to?"

"Making a few moves before I take it in for the day."

"Sounds good so are you coming stay by me tonight or do you want me to come to you?"

"I was thinking you can come to the crib around seven. I'll cook for you, and we can watch a movie."

"Sounds good to me. I'll see then."

"Fa sho shawty."

Once I ended the call with Slugga, I finally pulled out of the mall parking lot. It was a little after three in the afternoon, so I went home. I went upstairs to pack me an overnight bag, then came back down and heated up some of the leftovers from last night. After I had finished eating, I went back upstairs to take a shower and a nap. I was definitely gonna need all of my energy for what I had in mind for my boo tonight.

The sound of the rain tapping against the window is what woke me up. Looking at the time I got up to go freshen up and get dressed. I was about to slip something on when I got an idea. I decided to put the lingerie on and just wear my raincoat over it. I made sure I had everything I needed packed in my bag and zipped it up. I put my bag on my shoulder, grabbed my purse, phone, keys, and left out of my room closing my door behind me. I could hear E talking as I was walking down the stairs but since I didn't hear another voice, I knew she was on the phone.

"Good night, friend. I'm about to go to Slugga's."

"One sec baby." She said putting Lynx on hold. "Be careful out there and let me know when you make it."

"I will friend." I responded before leaving out and locking up behind me. On cue she was looking out the window watching me walk to my car.

I carefully drove to Slugga's crib and made it there in about forty-five minutes. I spritzed myself with Strawberries & Cream body spray before grabbing my stuff and getting out. I knocked on the door and waited for him to answer.

"Who is it?"

"It's me."

"Me who?" He asked but before I could respond he was unlocking the door and stood in the doorframe with a smirk. "Sup shawty?" He removed my bag from my shoulder and pulled me into a hug kissing me on the lips.

"Hey you." I finally spoke once the kiss ended. He stepped aside allowing me to walk inside. He closed the door and locked up behind us. Then he reached for my purse and took it along with my bag to his room. I stood in the middle of the living room waiting for him to come back where I was so I could make my move. As soon as I heard his footsteps getting close, I started unbuttoning my raincoat.

"Damn Shawty!" He mumbled with lust-filled eyes as he took in my full appearance. Dropping the raincoat onto the floor it formed a puddle near my feet, and I did a sexy little spin so he could get a complete view. I was truly appreciative of the fact my bruises had faded and were no longer visible otherwise I wouldn't have come to this man's house half naked. "I see what you on, but you know a nigga cooked you dinner. Let's eat first."

"How about you turn the food on warm and we'll eat later after we work up an appetite?" I replied with a smirk of my own. He nodded and went into the kitchen to do what I requested.

"I hope you know what you're getting yourself into." He tossed out before scooping me up and carrying me into his bedroom laying me in the center of his bed.

Slugga stripped down and my eyes bulged out of the socket when they landed on his dick. This nigga was the size of a toddler, and I knew my face displayed the disappointment, yet he didn't seem bothered or ashamed. I knew I couldn't turn back now or hurt his feelings, so I guess I gotta see this shit through. He climbed in bed positioning his body between my legs and his lil man grazed my skin. Slugga began kissing me and I kissed him back slipping my tongue in his mouth. The kiss was so deep and passionate I almost forgot he was packing a baby dick. He pulled away to give my titties some attention, before easing down to my freshly shaved pussy.

There are no words to describe the tongue lashing this man gave me coupled with the minty freshness of his breath, I damn near drowned him with all of my juices. Things took an interesting turn when he rose up and reached over me, going in his nightstand to grab a rubber and I saw the gold Magnum wrapper. In my mind I'm thinking he don't have enough dick for that and it's gonna come off and get lost in my pussy. Before I could object, I watched him roll it onto the anaconda standing tall before me. This nigga was a grower and not a shower, now I'm wondering where he's about to put all that. The mushroom head along was enough to make a bitch abort the mission, but the curve, girth, and length piqued my curiosity, so I definitely was gonna at least try it out.

"Sssssss!" I sounded like a damn snake when he eased the head in, and I wanted to cry because it felt like he was ripping my insides apart.

"You good shawty?" He questioned with genuine concern in his eyes, and I nodded. He took his time easing himself all the way inside of me, being very gentle, making sure I was completely comfortable. I was nervous and trembling like Betty Wright, but this is what I wanted, and tonight is the night.

U GOT IT BAD

LUXE MALVEAUX

It had been a few weeks since Juvie went to visit her pops and he called later that day to talk to me. He basically told me he knows all about me and if Juvie gets hurt once she finds out the truth that he was gonna have my tongue and dick delivered to my mom's house. As a man I can't do nothing but respect it but at the same time I fear no man. I had actually been contemplating telling her the truth but at the same time I just feel confessing now would destroy what we have, and I just can't take that risk.

"You good baby? You look like something is bothering you?"

"I'm good lil mama. Are you ready for today?" I asked looking into her eyes changing the subject.

"As ready as I'll ever be." She let out a deep sigh.

"Don't be so hard on yourself it's no different than any of your other first days of school."

"If you say so. My biggest fear is getting lost on campus." I chuckled because she has been terrified of starting college. I'm just glad she chose to go to a HBCU close by. I made it my duty to take her to school on her first day, so I came by this morning and of course she had breakfast waiting on a nigga. Rissa was at Slugga's and would meet up with her later since they're classes started at different times.

She went upstairs to get her backpack and stuff. I took the backpack and her books from her before we stepped outside, as I stood waiting for her to lock the door. Once we both were settled in the truck I pulled off and made my way towards Airline Highway to get her to school on time for her first class. I held her hand as I drove rubbing the back of her it in an effort to ease her mind and remove the nervousness she was feeling.

"Text me before your last class ends and where you want me to pick you up and I'll be here." I told her once I had pulled up in front of Higgins Hall for her history class.

"Ok baby, thank you for taking the time out to make sure my first day went by smoothly."

"What I told you about that? I got you no matter what."

"I know baby and that's why I love you." She leaned over to kiss me.

"I love you too lil mama. Now go have good first day and I'll see you later." I told her kissing her soft lips again before she grabbed her stuff and got out. My baby is majoring in Criminal Justice and I'm so fucking proud of her.

I had a meeting with Slugga. It had been a few weeks since I had put some work in his hands and that nigga was getting off that shit quicker than a muthafucka and my bread was always right. With Slugga on my team that put me in position to slang nothing but weight. I ain't wasting my time dealing with nickel and dime sales, that's what I got street runners for. This also gave me more time to maintain my hectic lifestyle and spend more time with my kids. I had been thinking about leaving UPS and going drive somewhere else, so I was gonna go put in a few applications at Mockler Beverage, Budweiser, and probably Kleinpeter.

After I finished handling my business it was almost two in the afternoon. I was gonna grab a bite to eat but decided against it since Juvie would be finishing up with her last class soon and is probably hungry too. So, I went hollered at my patna, Chunky to kill time til I had to go pick her up.

"What's up my nigga?" I yelled out the window when I pulled in his driveway before he made it inside his house.

"Sup my nigga bouta to go in here and burn one. You wanna match one?"

"Hell yeah!" I parked and grabbed my smoke, Zig Zags, and phone before hopping outta my truck and following him inside.

"What you been up to my nigga? I ain't seen you in a minute."

"Shit between work, Juvie, Miranda, and the kids my free time be limited as fuck." I told him as I rolled up two joints.

"Damn, nigga you still fucking with the lil chick Juvie?"

"You damn right that's my muthafuckin' baby man. I'm actually waiting on her to get out of her last class so I can scoop her up."

"That's what's up. Class? I thought you said she was graduating a few months ago."

"Nigga, she did! My baby started her classes at Southern today."

"Oh shit, got you a college girl now. You ain't worried she gonna leave you for one of them niggas on the yard."

"Do I look worried? See you ain't never met Juvie that's why you asking me that bullshit. Trust me I got that on lock."

"She still don't know you're married?"

"Nope but check this shit out! Matter of fact hit the weed first cause I'm bout to fuck your head up with this one." I passed him the joint I had just fired up and waited for him to take a few pulls before I spoke. "Guess who her daddy is?"

"Nigga how I'm gonna guess that shit and I don't even know who she is." He said hitting the joint again passing it to me and finish rolling his blunt.

"Prime."

"Prime? Deion Sanders her daddy? Damn you done hit the jackpot nigga?"

"Bruh I know you ain't that fucking high. Besides, Deion Sanders name is Prime Time fool. Hell no, nigga Scotlandville Prime." That nigga eyes widened as he dropped the weed, he was stuffing into the cigar.

"How the fuck you just finding that shit out and what you gone do?" I ran the whole story down about the visit and the phone call. "Man, you gone have to blow in her booty, so she don't tell her daddy on you, especially when she find out about Miranda."

"Nigga what?"

"I'm just saying you gonna have to go above and beyond to keep her happy, so she don't have shit bad to report to her pops or your ass is grass my nigga."

"I ain't worried about that man. Like I told you I got that on lock."

"I hear ya bruh. Nigga is you gonna ever grow up and start rolling blunts. Over here matching with joints like this the eighties and shit."

"Nigga fuck you. My papers smoke just like cigars you a high muthafucka ain't ya?"

"I'm definitely high."

We shot the shit a few more minutes when Juvie text me to let me know she would be outta class soon.

"Aight my nigga that's my lil mama right there. I'mma

holla at ya later." I told him dapping him up and grabbing my stuff so I could bounce.

"Be safe my nigga."

"Fa sho!" I was faded as fuck when I climbed back in my truck the weed and the beers had a nigga feeling just right. After popping in some old school, I pulled off and headed to the Subway on campus where she told me she would be waiting for me.

Twenty minutes later I was pulling into the Subway parking lot just as she walked up. Putting the truck in park I reached over, opening the door for her.

"Sup lil mama?" I told her as I looked her over. Them damn glasses; something about them glasses added to her beauty making my dick instantly brick up.

"Hey baby!" She hopped in leaning over to kiss me before putting her seatbelt on.

"So how was your first day?"

"It wasn't too bad, just a lot of walking since I didn't drive. I can't wait to get home and take a shower. The classes weren't too bad though."

"That's good. I told you there was nothing to worry about. You hungry?"

"Famished if I'm being honest."

"You wanna stop and grab something on the way to the house?"

"Nah, the least I can do is cook for you since you went out of your way to make sure I had a good day today."

"You don't have to do that Juvie. I know that sun probably drained you."

"It's early so I'm good. What do you have a taste for?"

"I'm not picky, you know what I eat, so it's up to you." I told her as I went through the light that turned red just as I made it under. Out of nowhere the red and blue lights appeared in my rearview signaling for me to pull over. "Fuck!"

"Just be cool baby." She said grabbing my smoke stash that I forgot to put up when I left Chunky's crib. Her movements were minimal as she slipped it in her panties so fast; if I wasn't sitting here watching I wouldn't have believed it. She pushed her glasses up on her nose making herself look even nerdier as she opened one of the textbooks on her lap while she pretended to read it.

The cop finally emerged from his vehicle tapping my window. "License and registration please." I wanted to ask why I was being pulled over, but I didn't wanna escalate the situation with Juvie in the truck with me, as well as the weed when I realized the cop was Bruh Stupid. You ain't from Baton Rouge if you don't know about that low down muthafucka.

"I pulled you over for running that red light back there." I nodded because technically I didn't, but I wasn't about to go back and forth with Bruh Stupid and he get to acting ignant out here. Juvie continued turning the pages in her book without saying a word she deserved an Oscar for this performance she was putting on. "I'll be back." He walked off with my shit going back to his car, I already know he ran my plate, and my shit was good. All he could do is just write me a ticket and let me go on about my business.

Bruh Stupid returned with the ticket, my license, and registration. "Here ya go and drive like you got some damn sense." I just nodded and put everything back up and drove off before he found some other reason to come fucking with me. I could have easily let that nigga have it but you gotta know which battles to pick. That nigga so grimy I knew not to even fuck with it, plus I know somebody who can take care of the ticket for me so I'm good either way.

"You good lil mama?" I asked once we had made it a good distance from where we were pulled over.

"Yeah, I'm straight. What about you?"

"I'm cool but you know you didn't have to do that?"

"Huh?"

"Juvie how many times I gotta tell you, if you can huh you can hear. I'm talking about the weed. I appreciate you for looking out, but you don't ever have to do no shit like that for me. I'm a man and can take my own lick if it ever come down to it. I let her know off the rip I'm not that type of nigga but at the same time that shit made a nigga feel good. If I ever doubted her love for me before which I never did, I know for a fact she loves me and got my back if don't nobody else do.

"Baby, I'm gonna go shower first then I'll cook, if that's alright with you." She said as soon as we made it inside of her crib. I nodded my head as I followed her up the stairs to her bedroom. Food was the last thing on my mind as thoughts of feasting on her ran through my head. I watched her as she maneuvered around her room before going into the bathroom. I was high, horny, and my dick was harder than a muthafucka, so I stripped down til I was wearing nothing but my socks and climbed in her bed.

"Baby why are you in my bed?" She questioned when she walked back into the room wearing just a towel.

"Shit come over here and find out." I replied tossing the covers off of me so she could see what was awaiting her.

"Damn!" She mumbled biting her bottom lip as she glided over to me and climbing onto my lap. I undid the towel tossing it on the floor before removing her glasses and carefully sitting them on the nightstand. Her perky titties made my mouth water as her nipples stared at me looking like two Hershey's Kisses.

“Come sit my pussy on my face.” I commanded as I laid back with my hands behind my head.

“Your pussy huh?” She asked cocking her head to the side.

“You know that’s all me that’s why you came in here with nothing but a towel on.”

“I came in here to get dressed so I can go cook.”

“Juvie fuck that food right now.” I’m tryna eat something else and when I get done with her ass, she won’t have the energy to cook any damn way.

CATER 2 U

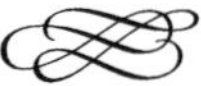

EUPHORIA GUIDRY

I'm finally at a point where I feel as if I'm managing school, work, and my relationship without being overwhelmed. I quit McDonald's and ended up at Footlocker which worked out better, since they were more accommodating with my school schedule plus I love shoes. It was November and Fall break was right around the corner and I welcomed it. I had just got off work and was headed to my evening class even though I would rather be going home and cuddle up with my man.

Once I made it on campus, I searched for a parking spot and luckily, I found one close by, so I didn't have far to walk. After double checking and making sure I wouldn't be towed or booted, I parked and got out before walking across the street to TT Allain, the building my class is in. When I made it to my math class, most of my classmates were in their seats but our professor was out. I noticed everyone scribbling fast in their notebooks and I finally glanced at a note on the board stating class was cancelled for the remainder of the week and a list of assignments that must be completed when class resumes next Monday. Talk about a life saver cause I really didn't wanna be bothered today. After I had written my assignments in my binder, I speed walked my ass outta class so fast and quickly to where I parked. As soon as my ass hit the seat of my car, I started it so I could turn the a/c on since it was still warm this time of year and called Lynx.

"Sup lil mama, shouldn't you be in class?" He asked as soon as he answered the phone.

"Hey baby, that's actually why I was calling you my class was cancelled for the remainder of the week."

"Is that right? So, what you about to get into?"

"About to head home and see if Rissa's there. I know they had court this morning so I wanna see how that went. Besides that, cook and start on some of my homework. Why, you coming see me?"

"Oh yeah, I hope that shit went by smoothly for her. Juvie you know a nigga always wanna see you. What you cooking today?"

"I got a taste for lasagna. So that with a green salad and garlic bread."

"Damn that sounds good. I'll be there as soon as I finish handling this business. You need anything?"

"All I need is you."

"You know I got you. See you in a minute, love you."

"Ok baby, love you too." I sat my phone in the cupholder after we ended our call and pulled off so I could go home.

After stopping at Hi Nabor to get some ground beef, I went straight home. I didn't see Rissa's car in the parking lot when I got home so I made a mental note to call her as soon as I got inside and settled. I put my stuff down and called Rissa to check up on her and see how things went. She just said Brandon pleaded not guilty which her lawyer had already prepared her for so she wouldn't be caught off guard and make any loud outbursts or anything that would cause her to be held in contempt. She assured me she was good and was about to go out to eat with Slugga and we ended our call.

Once I got settled inside, I went in the kitchen to start cooking because if I showered first, I would be too relaxed and calling Lynx to bring me some food. While the meat was browning, I made my sauce from scratch. I drained the meat before adding it to my sauce and then started layering the lasagna before popping it in the oven. Next, I prepared the salad and put it aside so I could make the garlic bread, I'll pop it in the oven once Lynx called and let me know he's on his way here. I turned the oven on warm and went upstairs to shower.

As soon as I stepped out of the shower, I could hear my phone ringing. I already knew it was my boo because I heard his ringtone. I did my face routine and moisturized my skin before going into my room and slipping on a t-shirt, leggings, and slid my feet into my furry slippers. I grabbed my phone and called Lynx back.

"Hey babyyyy!" I sang out when he answered.

"Sup lil mama?"

"Nothing just got outta the shower what's up?"

"Oh yeah, so you got it ready for me huh?"

"It's always ready for you." I flirted back.

"And on that note, I'll be there in about fifteen minutes."

"See you then baby." I ended the call and went downstairs to start my homework while I waited for him. I got up after about ten minutes to put the garlic bread in the oven and rolled up a blunt. For some reason smoking helps me focus better. I was just about to spark it up when there was a knock on the door.

"Who is it?" I called out as I got up to go answer it.

"Your forever!" Lynx replied and I opened the door grinning like a Cheshire cat. "Sup lil mama?"

He wrapped his arms around my waist and walked me backwards inside using his foot to close the door. Using one hand, he reached behind him to lock it as he placed a kiss on my forehead. Then he kissed the tip of my nose, next he teased my lips with his tongue before inserting it into my mouth. We kissed as if we hadn't seen each other in weeks.

"A nigga been waiting all day to do that." He huskily stated once we had pulled apart and came up for air.

"Oh, you must've really missed me." I teased.

"Juvie you know a nigga miss you anytime we not together."

"I know I missed you too, that's why I called you as soon as I found out class was cancelled." I told him as I went to take the bread out of the oven. "You wanna hit this before we eat?" I asked him since I still had the blunt in my hand.

"Shit, you know I always wanna hit that."

"I'm talking about the weed you freak."

"My bad but yeah we can." I lit the blunt and took a few pulls before passing it to him and went into the kitchen. After washing my hands, I started making our plates and put them on the table.

"What you wanna drink baby?" I called from the kitchen while getting the glasses out.

"You got some brown in there?"

"Yeah Amaretto, Hennessy, and Remy."

"Mix me up some of that Amaretto and pineapple juice since a nigga gotta go to work in the morning."

"Ok." I mixed up our drinks and brought them to the table and he passed the blunt to me before he went to the bathroom. After taking about four good pulls I put it out, said my grace, and dug into my food.

"Damn Juvie you wasn't gonna wait on me."

"I'm sorry but I am starving and have been wanting this all day."

"I guess I'll let you slide." He sat across from me, blessed his food, and started eating.

"This ain't no spaghetti sauce out the jar."

"Never!"

"You just really the total package, probably know how to make biscuits from scratch too huh?" I winked at him as I continued to chew my food.

Once I was done eating, I started cleaning the kitchen while he ate seconds. He brought me his plate just as I washed the last dish. "I'm good and full now. You know a nigga really trust you for me to eat your lasagna."

"Really, why is that?" I asked confused.

"A nigga gotta be careful when it comes to women and red sauce." I just nodded since I had no earthly idea what he was talking about.

"You want some more to drink?"

"Yeah, I got it though. You want another too?"

"A little, I got class in the morning though."

After he had fixed our drinks and passed me the glass and grabbed the remote to the stereo system. He went to see if our favorite CD, R Kelly's *Chocolate Factory* was one of the five discs in the CD changer before taking a seat on the end of the couch, I was stretched out on the couch reading my history chapters. Placing my feet in his lap he began to massage them as he relit the blunt. We passed it back and forth until it was all gone. The effects of the weed and liquor soon took over, next thing I knew we were in an intense tongue wrestling match. One thing led to another, and we somehow ended up on the floor naked as two jaybirds while he savagely beat my kitty up. We were in our own lil world when suddenly the locks turned and before we could even cover ourselves with the throw blanket I kept on the couch, Rissa had walked in. He jumped clean out of me, grabbed his pants, and took off down the hall.

"Oh shit! My bad y'all!" Rissa giggled as she walked back out and closed the door behind her.

Lynx emerged from the bathroom wearing only his pants and one sock. We looked at each other and busted out laughing as we hurriedly got dressed, making ourselves decent. After about five or six minutes there was a knock on the door.

"Come in!" I called out since I knew it was Rissa.

"Unt! Unt! Are y'all freaks dressed?" Rissa questioned.

"Yeah, friend we're good." The door opened and in walked Rissa and Slugga who both wore huge grins. Nobody said anything as we all looked around at each other, then Rissa finally spoke addressing the elephant in the room.

"My bad for interrupting y'all fuck fest." And we all fell out laughing. Shit I was high and tipsy, so everything was funny to me right now. I let them know I had cooked, while Lynx and I gathered our things before going up to my bedroom. "It must've been really good my friend running upstairs to finish." Rissa crazy ass yelled out causing everybody to bust out laughing again.

We made it up my room and I stripped down before climbing in my bed. Lynx put the R Kelly CD back on, before stripping down, and getting in bed next to me. Pulling me into his arms we just talked about my plans for Fall break which was literally two weeks away. I then told him my aunt had just bought a house in Baker and they were having a housewarming party this Saturday afternoon and we made plans for that night since it's been a minute since we've went out and did anything due to our hectic schedules.

"You ready to finish what we started downstairs?" He asked as he nuzzled his nose into my neck before sucking on it. I'm pretty sure there'll be a hickey there as usual. He loves sucking on my neck knowing it's gonna leave a mark instantly.

Lynx rolled me over til I was sitting on top of his semi-erect dick as he massaged my titties tweaking my nipples. I threw my head back as the pleasure took over my body as I slowly rotated my hips rubbing my moist slit against his shaft making his dick come all the way alive beneath me. R Kelly had just started singing *Forever* when he lifted me up so he could enter me, and I swear he tickled my lungs cause he damn sure snatched my breath away. We began moving our bodies in sync with the music as I slowly rode him while he matched me stroke for stroke.

"Damn Juvie! Ride your dick ma!" Something about the way he said that set my entire body on fire.

The room was filled with so much passion as he met me thrust for thrust. Pelvis to pelvis the magnetic energy surrounding us was at an all-time high and if at all possible, strengthening our already strong bond. Something about this moment felt too good to be true and once again that feeling that something bad was going to happen came over me. I paused momentarily and shook my head to rid it of the negative thoughts attempting to invade my brain.

"You good lil mama?" I nodded not wanting to damper the mood with my thoughts. He flipped me over so that he was now on top yet still inside of me.

His strokes were slow and deep as he stared intensely into my eyes. "Oooohhhh Lynx, right there." I moaned out in ecstasy.

"You like that?"

"Yesssssssssssss! Oohhh shit Lynx you're in my stomach!" I panted out.

"You want me to stop?"

"Pleassseeee don't stop!" I begged since I was on the verge of cumming.

"Go ahead and cum for me Juvie." He commanded as I did Kegels on his dick. "Juvie don't move." I froze like a block of ice cause I knew if I moved he would nut before me, then my ass would be in trouble for the rest of the night and neither one of us had that kind of time.

Once he had gathered himself, he commenced to stroking me as if he had a purpose and a point to prove. I was throwing it back keeping up with his thrusts cause I would never let him outdo me. The intensity of his strokes as he pounded against my spot, I knew I would soon be erupting like a volcano.

Lynx hit me with a few more of those long, deep strokes and he got just what he wanted I wet his ass up. "Damn Juvie!" He pulled out and motioned for me to turn over so he could hit it from the back and boy did he hit it. When I felt his warm nut filling me up, I realized he wasn't wearing a rubber. I hopped up so quick and ran to the bathroom to pee and try to push as much of his nut outta me before hopping in the shower.

"I told your hot ass a nigga pull out game ain't shit!" Lynx said joining me in the shower. We both were so exhausted afterward we couldn't do shit but cuddle and fall asleep after we quickly changed the sheets and he set an alarm for him to go home and get dressed for work.

I CAN TELL

NARISSA TAYLOR

Slugga and I had just pulled up to my house after taking Jahzelle to see *The SpongeBob SquarePants* movie. I just needed to grab my books so I can finish writing my paper for my English class while at his crib. I saw E's car and Lynx's truck in the parking lot, so I knew they freaky asses were home. We parked and I got out as Slugga helped Jahzelle out. I stuck the key in turning the locks and counted to thirty in my head before I opened the door. I didn't need any more surprises I couldn't get the image of Lynx's naked ass outta my head fast enough.

When I opened the door E, Lynx, and Lulu were sitting at the table eating pizza when Jahzelle took off full speed to the table.

"Cuzzy, Cuzzy!" She screamed as she went over to hug LuLu! E and I both looked at each other in confusion while these two niggas looked like they both had swallowed a fucking canary and LuLu was clapping in excitement as she hugged Jazelle back.

"What the fuck is going on?" I thought I was asking the question in my head until E responded.

"Same thing I wanna know!" She said as she sat back in her chair with her arms folded grilling Lynx.

"Are one of y'all gonna tell us what just happened?" I asked looking between Lynx and Slugga while they failed at making eye signals to each other.

"Look Shawty it's not what y'all think."

"Not what we think but it looks like y'all have been pretending not to know each other."

"Look Juvie the girls are cousins. LuLu's mama is Jahzelle's great-aunt." Lynx finally spoke looking directly at E.

"And y'all couldn't tell us that or is there something else y'all hiding."

"Nah lil mama that's it. To be honest we didn't tell y'all because at the time Slugga hadn't told Rissa about Jahzelle so we just didn't say anything. Time passed us by that we basically forgot until now. "I apologize lil mama." He said reaching over and grabbing her hand and that bitch turned into putty in that nigga's hand.

"I guess I can forgive you too." I side-eyed Slugga and he let the breath out that he was holding.

"Y'all want some pizza E offered."

"I'm actually still pretty full from the popcorn and nachos at the movies. Y'all want some pizza." I asked Slugga and Jahzelle who was now standing by us again and they both declined. "Well, let me run upstairs and get my stuff and we can be on our way."

Once I got everything I needed, we said our goodbyes, and left them to enjoy the rest of their evening. If somebody would have told me that E and I would be in healthy relationships and playing step mamas, I would have called them every lie in the damn book but here we are. The ride to Slugga's house was quiet aside from the music as we were both lost in her thoughts. I know I told him I forgave him but there was a nagging feeling there was something they wasn't telling us. Like my grandmother always says, *"What's done in the dark always comes to the light,"* so if they're hiding something it'll come out eventually.

"You wanna stop and get something to eat before we get to the house?" Slugga queried interrupting my thoughts.

"Yeah, that's cool."

"What you gotta taste for?"

"Burgers or tacos is cool with me. Jahzelle what do you wanna eat?" I turned around to ask her opinion.

"Tacos!" She screamed.

"Tacos it is!" Slugga announced as he drove to the nearest Taco Bell.

We finally made it to Slugga's and I wanted to shower first that way I can eat and write my paper at the same time. After handling my business in the bathroom, I got dressed in some pajama pants, the matching tank top, and some colorful toe socks. I grabbed my books and went back into the living room taking a seat at the desk in the corner and powering Slugga's desktop computer on.

"You ready to eat Shawty?"

"Yeah bae."

"I got you." He went in the kitchen and heated up my crunchy tacos and crunched them up in a bowl adding sour cream and hot taco sauce just the way I like it. He passed me the bowl, fork, and napkin and glass of cranberry grape juice.

"Thank you!" He nodded before announcing he was about to get Jahzelle ready for bath time so we could watch a movie with her before bed. I loved how she included me in everything. A lot of little girls aren't too fond of sharing their daddies with another woman especially one that isn't their mama.

I had about three pages of this paper remaining, good thing I had already done the research so all I had to do was type it up and I would be done. I worked on my paper until Jahzelle and Slugga had both taken their baths and were seated on the couch waiting on me to watch the movie. So, I took a break to join them and as soon as the movie was over, I jumped back into it. A little after midnight my paper was finished and Slugga and I laid in bed talking about my upcoming court date.

"I'll be so glad when this is over, and I can put it behind me once and for all." I sighed in frustration.

"I understand how you feel shawty. It's like every court date you have to relive it and I know it fucks with your mental."

"Yes, you definitely hit the nail on the head."

"It's ok to not be ok all the time when it comes to that situation. That was a traumatic experience, and your healing process has been nothing short of amazing."

"That's because I have the best support system." I winked before pulling his face into mine pecking his lips a few times which led into a full-blown make-out session.

"Aight nah don't start nothing you can't finish shawty."

"When have I ever not been able to finish something, I started?" I retorted with a raised eyebrow and a smirk.

I talked a lot of shit knowing I'd be walking funny the next day. It's something about going to see a man about a horse and a horse is really there. That idiom was nothing short of the truth when it comes to Slugga's well-endowed ass.

"Come on let's get some sleep shawty." He tossed out after I yawned.

"Sleep?"

"Yeah, you're sleepy and I don't want no sleepy pussy." He mumbled with his eyes closed.

"Negro yo' ass is sleepy too." I giggled loudly.

"Hell yeah, a nigga tired but I promise once I get a few hours in me, I'll wake you up."

"If you don't I'll be waking you up. Good night bae!"

"Good night shawty, I love you." His response totally caught me off guard and I had to raise the fuck up to make sure I had heard him correctly. He started snoring as soon as I parted my lips to ask him to repeat what he had said.

Was it too soon for him to reveal that he loves me? Should I tell him I feel the same way or wait to confirm that he meant to say that. All of these questions rapidly ran through my mind as I wondered if this was another pivotal moment in our relationship. I honestly had been fell in love with him but never said anything because I felt it was too soon and didn't want to run him off. I always made sure my actions let him know I did, even though I have never verbally expressed it.

To say I was just yawning a few minutes ago, a bitch was wide awake all because this man said he loved me which I haven't even confirmed how he feels yet. Maybe I heard him wrong. Nah, he definitely said, *I love you.* And just like that my brain has gone into overdrive and about to overthink shit for no absolute reason at all, except I have no control of my brain, it has a mind of its own, pun intended.

I pulled out my phone and texted E to see what she thought about the situation, but the bitch didn't respond. Knowing them freaks she probably over there in a dick coma or got Lynx's dick buried down her throat. After going back and forth with my thoughts for about forty-five minutes my eyes finally got heavy. The yawns got faster and soon I was curled up under Slugga lightly snoring.

The next morning after breakfast while Slugga and I were cleaning the kitchen I casually brought it up. I asked him if he was just sleep talking, or did he remember what the last thing was he said to me before falling asleep. My stomach fell to my ass when he repeated his exact words, yet my heart smiled. Seeing that we were both on the same page with our feelings we went to get ourselves and Jahzelle ready so we could get our Sunday funday started before it was time for him to take her home.

NEVER KEEPING SECRETS

LYNX MALVEAUX

Of all the houses in Baker, Juvie's aunt had to buy the one right fucking next to me. I had just pulled into my driveway with Miranda and the kids when I noticed her car parked next door. She and a few other girls who I assumed were her cousins or something walked out of the house just as I had got outta the truck. Our eyes locked as I silently pleaded with her to just keep walking. Apparently, it worked because she stared for a few moments before she turned her head. I couldn't read her expression and that actually had a nigga shook. She kept walking until they were at the edge of the driveway where her car was parked. I prayed she didn't see Miranda but that prayer ain't get no higher than my thoughts cause as soon as Miranda hopped her happy jack ass out, Juvie turned around. My heart was beating out of my chest because I didn't know how this shit was gonna play out and I was trying to get my story together just in case the shit hit the fan.

I grabbed LuLu outta her car seat while she opened the door for LJ to get out on his side. We had just made it home from the grocery store and I knew I had to get the bags outta the truck. I had to get my story straight and it had to be airtight cause this is totally different than a phone call to her job. The only thing saving my ass right now is that she never told anyone in her family about me, so I know that's why she isn't saying anything but if looks could kill this would be my final chapter in this book.

"Here get LuLu, so I can start grabbing these bags." I told Miranda passing her LuLu who was knocked out sleep.

"LJ go help your daddy."

I passed him a few of the light bags and sent him into the house. Even though it's been a minute since he's seen Juvie, I didn't need him recognizing her. I tried to carry as many bags as I could in as few trips as possible, so I can get the hell away from here. As soon as I brought the last of them in the house, I told Miranda I would be back and got the fuck on down. The only person who could help me at this moment was my mama, so that's where I was headed. I know she gone cuss my black ass out cause she been told me to tell Juvie the truth, but for some reason I just could never do it. A nigga like me that ain't really scared of shit, the thought of losing Juvie got my chest tight.

Ten minutes later I was pulling up to mama's crib parking behind her car. I sat in my truck for a minute before I finally got out. She had the door open waiting for me. "Hey mama." I spoke as I gave her a hug.

"Hey son. What's wrong?" Damn was it that obvious. I swiped my hand over my face as I stepped inside closing the door behind me and locking it. "Well?" She questioned with her hands on her hips.

"You might wanna sit down for this."

"Oh Lord. What you done got yourself into nah?"

I told her the whole story and her eyes turned to slits as she just stared at me. "Well son, I don't know what you expect me to say cause I told you to tell her the truth in the beginning. Juvie is a feisty lil something and whatever happens is your own fault. Prolonging the situation only makes it worse when the truth is revealed. All I can say is good luck cause you're gonna need it." She got up and left me sitting there alone, just me and my thoughts. A nigga was fucking terrified to the point I was scared to call her.

"I'm gone mama!" I called out to her as I got up to leave. I locked up and hopped in my truck driving straight to Juvie's crib.

She wasn't home when I made it, but a nigga was prepared to wait as long as I had to. It was in that moment I knew for a fact I loved her more than Miranda. At this point I was willing to risk it all for Juvie, my marriage included.

It was a little after seven when I finally seen her car pulling into the complex. The fact that I'd been waiting for almost three hours didn't even bother me. I knew she was pissed because not once had she called or texted me. After she parked and got outta her car I did the same. It was either now or never.

"Sup Juvie?" I called her name to get her attention and she cocked her head to the side looking me up and down.

"Hey Lynx." Her reply was dryer than the Sahara plus she didn't call me baby. At least she spoke back so that gave me a little hope.

"Can I come in so we can talk about earlier?"

"Talk about earlier huh? Yeah, let's do that." She ordered turning on her heels and walking in the direction of her apartment and I followed close behind her.

I took a seat on the couch as soon as we made it inside and she sat on the other one facing me giving me her undivided attention.

"You said you wanted to talk, so talk." I didn't know how to handle Juvie talking to me like that cause it wasn't normal.

"I just wanna say what you saw you isn't what you think you saw, if that makes sense."

"That's the dumbest shit I ever heard so please enlighten me."

"Well, that's the kid's mama and she needed to go make groceries, which isn't easy with two small kids, so I took her. It's no big deal."

"That's it, so why didn't you just tell me that?"

"I don't know, plus I didn't expect to see you."

"I hear ya. Is there anything else I need to know?"

"Nah that's it lil mama. Now come over here and give me some love." I inwardly breathed a sigh of relief since she seemingly believed the story, I gave her.

I know should have just come clean, but I just couldn't do it. The love I have for her is too deep and I can't break her heart or risk her leaving me. She finally got up and came over to me and I pulled her onto my lap and hugged her tightly. I just needed to hold her to ensure our connection, our bond, was still intact. So, I scooped her up and carried her upstairs to her bedroom and laid her on her bed while I went in the bathroom to run her a bubble bath. A nigga was about to do whatever it takes to get back on her good side.

Once I had her water right, I went back in the room and carried her bridal style to the bathroom. Placing her on her feet, I carefully undressed her and put her in the tub. I grabbed the washcloth and gently washed her body twice before letting the water out so she could rinse under the shower. When she got out to do what she does to her face I was in the room wearing nothing but my boxers and socks ready to give her a full body massage. She was so relaxed she couldn't do nothing but curl up in the bed and go to sleep. I got up and took a shower before climbing in bed with her pulling her close and doing the same.

The next morning, I woke up to some of her superb, toe-curling head and that made me feel good. That act alone let me know everything between us was copasetic and that was all that mattered. We fucked and sucked until we had drained each other and ended up going back to sleep. It was after four in the evening when we woke up again and I left out to go grab us some food cause I know she didn't have the energy to cook us anything.

After making sure Juvie was good, I finally headed home. I already knew it was gonna be some bullshit since I didn't come home last night but I don't give a damn. It ain't like she is innocent cause she still couldn't tell me where she was going that day, I saw her flying up Plank Road. I know what I'm doing with Juvie is wrong and initially I felt bad but shit not no more. At this point I guess we both doing us.

When I pulled into my driveway, I sat in my truck smoking a joint before getting out and going inside to deal with hurricane Miranda. I sprayed and let my windows down to air my truck out before finally getting out. Sticking my key in the door, I opened it and stepped inside surveying the kitchen, I noticed pots on the stove and wasn't the least bit interested in their contents. I proceeded down the hall where I could hear Miranda and LJ in his room talking.

"But mama why can't we go see him today?" The wheels in my head began to turn as I wondered who he was so eager to go see. Instead of making my presence known something told me to listen a little further so I did.

"LJ, I promise I'll take you this weekend. Remember I told you those visits are a secret, and we have to be careful and not talk about them here."

"Yes ma'am, I just like hanging with him."

"I know mama is gonna figure something out and soon." She replied and before I could move, she stepped out of his room and was met with my presence.

Her face displayed immediate shock as if she had seen a ghost. "When did you get home?" I guess she was trying to see how much I had heard but I wasn't about to divulge that information just yet.

"I just walked in the door, why?"

"No reason since you left here yesterday and never returned nor called. So where in the hell have you been?" She questioned through her teeth.

"Wherever you were that day you lied about being at work."

"Really Lynx, why do you keep bringing up that fake ass story you concocted." She tossed over her shoulder as she walked in the direction of our bedroom.

"Sup son?" I stuck my head in LJ's room speaking to him.

"Hey." He responded dry as hell which wasn't like him at all, and I made a mental note to ask him about it later. I went in LuLu's room to check on my baby girl, who was in her bed knocked out sleep and lightly snoring. After kissing her on her forehead I went in the bedroom to finish dealing with Miranda before getting in the shower.

"You know there's nothing fake or concocted about that shit you just haven't come up with a lie yet."

"Why do you always try to flip the script on me when I call you out on your bullshit?"

"Ain't nobody flipping shit. You asked a question and I responded with a question of my own."

"Like I said flipping the damn script."

"I'll answer your questions when you can answer mine." I told her and walked off to start the shower.

"Hmmph, and the first thing you do is take a shower

when you come home. You must think I'm stupid or something."

"I could say the same about you."

"Whatever Lynx I'm not about to argue with you over your dirt. I cooked; I'll make your plate when your done in the bathroom."

"I'm not hungry so no need to do that." Miranda must be smoking crack if she thinks I'm about to eat some shit she cooked and she just called herself tryna check a nigga about not coming home. I'll eat a fried bologna sandwich before I eat what's in them damn pots, fuck that shit.

While in the bathroom, I replayed Miranda and LJ's conversation in my head and the way he spoke to me. Something was up and I needed to get my son alone to find out what the fuck is going on and fast.

WEAK

EUPHORIA GUIDRY

Thanksgiving break had come and gone, and it was nice. Rissa and I cooked a small dinner just so we would have food at our crib after we were done visiting our families. This was our first year attending Bayou Classic as students and Lynx and Slugga made it a weekend to remember. From the Greek Show & Battle of the Bands to the game and a whole lot of partying in between.

It's currently Christmas Eve and although things between Lynx and I are good, I'd be lying if I'd said something has been off ever since I'd seen him next door to my aunt's house. Granted I didn't go off on him while there or when he came over to talk later that day, I knew there was more to the story. For instance, he did tell me that was his baby mama, but he left out the part that her name was Miranda. It all came to me when I saw her face and I remembered something that caught my eye a while ago. One night he was dropping me off at home after work, I noticed a badge on the floor of the Yukon with her picture and the name Miranda. I thought both vehicles were his and I could be wrong but for some reason I think the Yukon is hers and he was riding me around in that woman's truck. I've been trying to be more observant of Lynx, his actions, as well as asking the correct questions.

I had just finished wrapping the last of his gifts and placed it under the tree Rissa and I had decorated when my phone rang. I saw it was Lynx and answered it before it rolled to voicemail.

"Hey baby." I spoke as soon as I answered.

"Sup lil mama?"

"Nothing much just finished wrapping gifts and just about done cooking for tonight."

"Good cause a nigga is starving. I'm about to pull up in a sec. I'll call you to come out." We switched vehicles earlier because he said he needed to get my oil changed and get it detailed or something.

"Okay baby. I'll see when you get here, love you."

"Love you too, Juvie."

We hung up and I saw a text from Rissa letting me know her a Slugga were on the way with the drinks. The four of us had pulled names for Thanksgiving and we were gonna exchange all of our gifts, play games, smoke, drink and chill tonight. Our menu consisted of finger sandwiches, BBQ meatballs, chips and dip, and chicken and sausage gumbo. I arranged the food on the counter and made sure everything was covered before taking my seat back on the couch vibing to the music.

Ten minutes later Lynx was calling me back. "Helloooo!" I sang out.

"Come outside beautiful."

"I'm walking out right now I told him before hanging up and throwing my phone on the couch.

My mouth hit the floor the closer I got to my car because I just know I'm not seeing what I'm seeing. "Baby you didn't?" I squealed.

"Oh yes the fuck a nigga did, Merry Christmas Juvie!" He smiled as he leaned up against the trunk of my car.

"Thank you, baby!" I jumped in his arms kissing all over his face. His sneaky ass took my car and put some twenty-two-inch rims on it. My car was already fresh, but the upgraded rims just added to it and made it even more eye-catching. It wasn't too long ago I told him I was thinking about putting some bigger rims on my car and in true Big Lynx fashion it's already handled. See, it's shit like this that makes me believe he could do no wrong but like I said something was off about that baby mama situation. I'm not gonna bring it up and ruin our mood tonight but the conversation will definitely be revisited.

Once I was done admiring my car, he sat me on the trunk and grabbed a few gift bags out of my car before scooping me back up and carrying me inside. He sat me on the couch, locked the door and put the bags under the tree before taking a seat next to me. I grabbed his face and kissed him like it was my first time seeing him today.

"Oooooohhhhh bestie, them muthafucking rims is NICE!!!!" Rissa's crazy ass screamed when she busted in the house with excitement.

"I know huh friend my baby just surprised me with them for Christmas."

"Bro, you did your thang them thangs is nice."

"Yeah, bruh them bitches poppin'." Slugga added his input.

"Thanks, y'all know it ain't nothing off limits when it comes to my Juvie." I sat there blushing like a damn fool. This man spoils be in more ways than one and the materialistic shit is a bonus cause I've learned long ago, not to reject it or put up a fight.

"Y'all ready to get this party started." Rissa asked while

doing a lil two-step. I loved seeing my friend so happy despite all she's been through.

"Let's do it!" I told her getting up to make plates for Lynx and myself while Rissa did the same for her and Slugga. The guys were sitting around talking amongst themselves probably some street shit. They didn't even have a clue that we had figured out they were working together, and we won't ever bring it up. We just pray for their safety and that they always return home to us.

After we ate, we exchanged gifts before playing games by midnight we were all pretty much drunk and high as hell. Rissa and Slugga had left wanting us to have the house to ourselves. Lynx and I were lying in my bed just talking and cuddling and around a quarter to two he got up and start getting dressed. "Where are you going?" I yawned out in confusion.

"I'm gonna head to the crib so I can be home when my babies wake up in the morning to open their gifts." I don't know what it was about that sentence, but it was as if I had an epiphany. I instantly sobered up and a million thoughts ran through my head before I spoke again.

"Are you married?" I don't know where the hell the question came from, but Lynx froze, and he looked as pale as a ghost.

"Huh?"

"If you can huh, you can here." I used his own shit on him. Though, I had asked the question I was not prepared for what came out of his mouth next.

He stopped getting dressed and sat back on the bed swiping his hand over his face. "Yes."

"What the fuck did you just say to me?" I sat all the way up in bed making sure I heard this shit correctly.

"Yes, I'm married." His eyes glossed over, and I instantly became numb.

"So, you mean to tell me that I have unknowingly been a sideline chick.

"It's not what you think Juvie."

"The fuck you mean it's not what I think." I jumped out of bed getting in his face. "So let me guess the house next door to my aunt is y'all's house."

"Yeah." He whispered. I started laughing like a damn lunatic.

"So, you literally lived around the damn corner from me, and I had no clue. I gotta give it to you, you were smooth as hell with this shit. Why did you lie to me after I told you I was cheated on and here you got me in the same predicament? I went from the one being on cheated on to a fucking a mistress." My heart was broken, and I broke down in tears cause I felt bad, I would never want to put another woman in a position I had been in before.

"It's not what you think lil mama. Everything between us is real. The feelings I have for you are real. You mean more to me than she does and that's the God honest truth." I just continued sobbing uncontrollably. I was ugly crying, chest heaving up and down, just downright distraught. "I promise I'm gonna make this right."

I knew at this moment we were done as he kissed my tears away. I had already made up my mind to give him my body one last time. One thing led to another, and the next thing I knew he had entered me. As deep as our connection was when we made love this time it was different than any time before. I silently cried with each thrust, and it was like he knew we was over because I felt his tears mixing with mine. We nutted simultaneously and he filled me up with everything he had. Staring into each other's eyes we just laid there in silence. He kissed me on my forehead and then sealed it with a breath-taking kiss before pulling out of me.

Lynx got up and went in the bathroom to clean himself up before returning to clean me. The tears poured from my eyes as they slid over my ears soaking my pillow. He started to get dressed and I just stared at him intently wanting to embed him in my memories forever. I could literally feel my heart continuing to shatter with each article of clothing he put on and my stomach was in knots. When he was fully dressed, he turned back towards me. "I'll call you tomorrow and no matter what I love you Juvie. I'm gonna lock the door behind me. Merry Christmas." I nodded as my chest tightened when my so-called forever walked out of my bedroom door. I ugly cried until I had somehow managed to fall asleep.

The next morning, I woke up praying that last night was a nightmare but when I looked in the mirror and saw my swollen eyes from all of the crying, I knew that shit was real. As the conversation rolled through my head like a movie, the tears began to fall again, and I just wanted to skip Christmas and crawl back in bed. I wasn't in the mood to be around a bunch of jolly muthafuckas when my heart was just broken into a million fucking pieces. I shot a group text to my family and told them Merry Christmas and that I wasn't feeling good and would bring gifts when I'm feeling better and climbed back in bed pulling the covers over my head.

As much as I wanted to call Rissa and tell her I needed my best friend, I wasn't gonna ruin Christmas for her. Lynx had texted me telling me Merry Christmas and that he would come by later. Little did he know that would be a blank trip because I had no intention of getting out of bed, let alone answering the door for him.

Mentally my mind replayed our whole relationship trying to scour over every single detail to see if there were any clues

I missed. I wondered if his family knew I didn't know I was the other woman and if they were all laughing at me. I know I approached him, but he should have told me he was married from the jump, and I would have left him alone. The fact he didn't tell me and allowed me to fall weak in the knees in love with him hurt me to my fucking core. I wanted to scream, break things, just destroy shit, this was a hurt I'd never felt before nor would I wish it on my worst fucking enemy. This pain was foreign to me, and I don't know if I'd ever get over this shit. The connection and bond we share, man this shit is beyond devastating it's not like I can erase my feelings and love for him overnight, but I'm so hurt my soul is literally crying. In the blink of an eye, my happiness, my life was turned upside down, and what was weird is I still felt this crazy ass connection to the man who has caused me all of this turmoil. One thing for certain and two things for sure my heart will never beat for another man like it did for Lynx Malveaux. That man was my one true love even if it was all built on a lie with his super smooth and sneaky ass.

I had been lying in bed staring at the ceiling as the tears continued to roll down my cheeks when Rissa finally came home busting in my room. "Merry Christmas Bestie!" She screamed but I couldn't even find the words to reply. There was definitely nothing merry about this Christmas. "Wait you're crying. E what's wrong?" she asked once she came closer to me.

"H-h-he li-li-lied." I stammered and stuttered out the only words that I could form at the moment.

Bewilderment etched in her face she asked, "Who lied, Lynx?" I slowly nodded my head as a fresh batch of tears spilled from the corners of my eyes. Kicking her shoes off she climbed into bed with me and pulled me in for a hug. I know she was confused because we were all happy and having a good time less than twenty-four hours ago. "Friend, I understand you're upset right now but I can't help you if I don't know what's wrong. Did he put his hands on you or something cause I'll go fuck him up." I shook my head no.

After minutes of us just lying there in silence I finally spoke and told Rissa everything that had transpired in the wee hours of this morning. She rose up into a sitting position and just looked at me with her mouth wide open, it was now her turn to be speechless.

"E, are you sure that he said he's married?"

"I've never been more sure of anything in my entire life."

"I mean, how when were they separated or something. The nigga spent so much time with you when did he have time for her?"

"Nah, they're definitely not separated. The nigga was just that good with covering his tracks."

"Remember I told you I saw him at that house for Aunt Mal's housewarming?"

"Yeahhhhhh." She dragged her response out.

"Bitch that's their house. The nigga literally lived around the corner from me and would literally take ten to fifteen minutes to get to my house. The whole time I thought he stayed with Ms. Veronica and his ass was right under my damn nose. I guess that explains why both of his vehicles were never at his mama's house at the same time."

"So, wait bitch, the Yukon is the wife's truck?"

"Most definitely and was riding me around in that lady's shit on the regular. I'm so fucking dumb."

"Nah friend, you're not about to do that. This is all on his ass so there is no need to blame yourself."

"I wanna hate him so bad but I can't. I'm done with his ass though."

"Man, I was praising and rooting for this nigga and he's no different than the rest. Now that I think about it that's why he and Slugga didn't tell us they knew each other. I'm gonna cuss Slugga's ass out."

"Don't do that Rissa. Slugga is not the blame for Lynx's actions, and it wasn't his place to tell me anything. Lynx had more than enough opportunities to come clean and he chose to ride with his lie."

"Have you talked to him since."

"He called and texted saying he's coming over later, but I have no intentions of ever speaking to him again. So, please don't let him in if you're here when he comes."

"I got you friend, I'm gonna help you get through this."

"Friend, I don't even know how I'm gonna get over this? Lynx was my person but apparently, he's her person too." I trembled as tears started to fall again.

"It's definitely not gonna be overnight and it will take some time for your heart to heal. For as long as it takes, I got your back. I'm not defending him but maybe their marriage isn't what you think it was or there was some kind of disconnect. I'm just on the outside looking in but from what I've gathered that man not only loves you but is in love with you."

"Yeah, but why did he lie? He didn't even give me an option to choose how I wanted to deal with the situation. Though, I would have still ended it, but it's the principle. I'm going to hell for being a damn sideline chick."

"Friend stop being dramatic. You did nothing wrong in this situation, this is all on him. At the end of the day, he was the one committing adultery not you."

"OH MY GOD!!!!" I screamed out loud and dramatically as hell which caused Rissa to jump.

"What's wrong friend?" She asked with her hand on her chest.

"That dick, I'm gonna definitely miss that dick."

"Well, I hope you at least gave him a courtesy goodbye fuck before he left."

"I did friend, and it was different but good as hell. It's like we both knew without speaking that it was our last time."

"Damn. So, are you ready to get out of bed and go celebrate Christmas?"

"Nah, I already lied and told mama nem I'm sick. I'm not leaving this room."

"That's not good friend, besides you love Christmas."

"Correction, I used to love Christmas. Go celebrate with your family, I'll be here when you get back."

"Are you sure friend cause I can stay with you."

"Rissa go, don't let me spoil your day."

"On one condition, we have a movie night when I get home."

"Deal." I told her just so she would leave me alone to drown in my own tears.

"Alright friend I'll see you when I get back. Call me if you need anything." I nodded before rolling over to stare a new hole into the wall. Fuck Christmas, fuck love, and at this point fuck Lynx, I thought before eventually crying myself to sleep.

COUNT ON ME

NARISSA TAYLOR

Things had been so weird since E and Lynx's break up. My poor friend took a leave from work and literally stayed locked up in her room. We had a week left before Spring semester began and I needed my friend to get it together as soon as possible. Which is why I am on my way home to pull her out of that room for a day of pampering. I understand this shit with Lynx hit her hard and unexpectedly, but I needed my friend back. According to Slugga, that nigga is just as hurt and heart-broken as she is. In the past I would empathize and normally have his back, but he is the cause of all this shit and for that I have no sympathy. Only my friend can get sympathy from me.

It was almost eight in the morning when I pulled in our complex. I don't care how much she puts up a fight but she's getting out of this damn house if I have to drag her out kicking and screaming. As soon as I parked, I hopped out and went inside ready for the battle I knew awaited me. I went inside locking the door behind me and tossing my things aside before running upstairs and heading straight for her room. I didn't even bother knocking as I burst into her room and flipped the light switch on.

"Friend, wake up!" I loudly commanded and she didn't respond. "Come on E we have a busy day ahead of us.

"I don't have any plans and I'm not leaving this room."

"Euphoria Ka'Shay Guidry if you don't get your ass up and outta this bed I'm calling Ms. Karla and tell her all about you and Lynx's relationship."

"You wouldn't dare!"

"Try me bitch! I've allowed you to wallow in your sadness long enough and this shit is coming to an end today."

I grabbed her hand and pulled her out of bed and led her into the bathroom. Flicking the light on I made her stand in front of the mirror and she dropped her head."

"No bitch, pick your head up. Look at you E this ain't even your steelo. Hair all matted, skin all ashen and pale, probably ain't washed your ass since last year. I refuse to allow you to continuing losing yourself right before my eyes." Tears pooled in the corner of her eyes and mine as well.

"I know you're in a lot of pain, but life goes on and it's time you start to heal friend. I got you every step of the way. Normally, I would encourage you to get under a new nigga to get over the old one but that's not even healthy for you at this point. Can you please do me a favor?"

"What's that?"

"Can you please brush your teeth and wash your ass while I find you something to wear?"

"Fuck you bitch! I do not smell that bad."

"If you can't smell it that means it's worse than I thought and you're now immune to your funk." She fell out laughing and that meant the world to me. I don't know the last time I'd seen her smile let alone laugh. I left out of the bathroom to give her some privacy and went back into her room to strip her bed and put her sheets to wash. I grabbed some fresh linens and made her bed up before going into her closet and finding her something to wear. Since this bipolar ass Louisiana weather could change at any moment, I figured I couldn't go wrong with a pair of jeans, a Jordan t-shirt and the Jordans to match. I made sure I didn't pick anything that Lynx had bought for her since I didn't know how she would react to it.

I could hear the blow dryer going which was a good thing cause that poor head was looking a hot ass mess. I laid her clothes out and went in my own room to change my shoes. Since, the ones I had on didn't really go with my outfit they were just the ones I had at Slugga's house to put on. After switching my shoes, I could hear my phone ringing downstairs, so I quickly went to get it. Slightly out of breath and seeing it was my lawyer, I quickly answered. He was calling to let me know that Brandon's bitch ass had accepted a plea deal and the charge for first-degree feticide will be reduced to second-degree feticide with a maximum sentence of up to fifteen years as well as second degree battery with a maximum of up to five years and provisions. Though, I wanted his ass to spend the rest of his life in jail, I was already prepared that would most likely not happen especially since this was his first offense. After reminding me of our upcoming court date, I thanked him for the update and ended our call.

Ten minutes later E had finally brought her ass downstairs looking ten times better than before. "You ready to hit the streets friend?"

"Yeah, cause I don't need you telling my mama all my damn business. Can we stop so I can get a new phone?"

"I sure was gonna tell it and tell it all. What's wrong with your phone?"

"Nothing but it's the one Lynx bought me, and if I'm gonna get through this shit I figured a new phone is a good start." My friend's eyes got glossy, but she sucked that shit up and refused to let anymore tears fall. I know she was tryna put on a brave front for me but in actuality she didn't even have to do that. I swear I wanna beat that nigga's up for every tear she's shed over his lying ass.

"We can do that but first let's get some breakfast in you, go to our spa appointment, then after we can go to the mall for a little retail therapy, and you can get a new phone then."

After running down some of today's plans we were on our way. For breakfast, we went to Denny's on South Acadian Thruway since it was her favorite. Once we were seated, we placed our orders and just talked about random shit. I purposely avoided the topic of relationships. I just wanted to be there for her like she has been there for me during my whole ordeal with Brandon. I filled her in on what the lawyer had called and said earlier, and she promised to go to court with me.

Once the waitress returned with our food, her stomach growled loud as hell. "Bitch when was the last time you ate?"

"I ain't really ate nothing since last year." She responded imitating David Ruffin on The Temptations movie followed by a wide smile. For some reason, I believed she was telling the truth and I instantly felt like shit for not making her eat and drink. The damn girl probably dehydrated for all I know.

At first, she was just picking over her food and I encouraged her to eat and before I knew it, she was scraping the plate with her fork. I told her to order more but she assured me she was full. I paid the tab, she covered the tip, and we left so we wouldn't be late for our spa appointment. For the remainder of our girls' day, she was in good spirits. We went to the nail salon after the spa, with a few more stops in between making the mall our last stop. We did some serious damage in there too, after we took our pictures of course. E was starting to get back to her old self and for me that was progress. She got her a new phone before we left the mall and was storing her contacts as I drove to our next destination.

Once we finally made it home before we got out the car to get the bags, she grabbed my hand and said, "Thank you so much for today friend. I didn't realize how much I needed to get out of the house and clear my head. I owe you one."

"You don't owe me shit. You're my best friend and I got you for life. Love you girl."

"That goes both ways love you too friend." She replied before reaching over the console and giving me a hug. "You ready to get all this stuff out the car?"

"Yeah, let's hurry up before it gets dark." We grabbed up all of our shit and had started to walk in the house when she suddenly paused, and I followed her eyes. She stared at her car and I'm pretty sure it was the rims that caught her attention. That was one of her Christmas gifts from Lynx which she received the same night their relationship came to an end. "You good friend?" I questioned with a raised eyebrow.

"Yeah, I'm good, just thinking about how fast shit can change in the blink of an eye. One minute I was surprised with gifts from a man that has always made me feel like the luckiest girl in the world and the next the minute the same man me feel like the dumbest girl in the world. God is funny like that." She chuckled shaking her head as she continued the short trek to our door.

I didn't have a response and I don't think I needed one. Her statement wasn't a conversation starter but more so of her coming to grips with her reality and saying it out loud to confirm it's real. We took all of our bags upstairs to our rooms and decided to make the rest of our night a movie night. E wanted to take her shower first, so I told her to go ahead while I ordered the pizza and rolled up the weed. I sent a quick text to Slugga thanking him again for being so understanding when I told him I needed a little space today to focus on my friend. He was the one who suggested we go get pampered and even paid for it. I gotta do something nice for him, I thought as I finished rolling two blunts and pulled out my phone to order our pizza and wings. I set the movie up and waited til she came down before going up to take my shower and put on something comfortable. We got high and pigged out watching movie after movie and ended up falling asleep on both couches.

THE LOVE WE HAD

The Love We Had Stays On My Mind

Lynx Malveaux

June 26, 2005

"Damn nigga you still walking around depressed and shit?" Chunky asked as soon as he hopped his ignant ass in my truck. "Ol' Allen Iverson still ain't fucking with ya?" I shook my head no as my mind drifted off to Juvie and the reason he calls her Allen Iverson, it was a few months ago but I remember that shit like it happened yesterday.

"Sup lil mama? What you up to?" I asked her as soon as she answered the phone.

"Hey baby. Nothing much just finished getting dressed waiting on Rissa's slow ass. What you up to?"

"I'm actually outside. Come out here for a sec I just stopped by to drop you off a lil something."

"Ok I'm walking out now." She said before hanging up."

"Act like you got some sense nigga when she comes out here." I told Chunky's retarded ass.

Not even a minute later she was walking in the direction of where I was parked. She had on this black skirt that stopped mid-thigh, with the matching black jacket, and some black boots that came up to her knees.

"Damn who the fuck is that?" Chunky mumbled.

"Nigga that's my muthafuckin' Juvie."

"Shit, I see why you stuck on that."

"Close your eyes nigga."

I opened the door and got out just as she made it to me. That was when I noticed the seventy-sixers logo on the right side of her jacket and the white skinny strap t-shirt underneath her jacket. My baby was so fucking beautiful and was wearing the fuck outta her lil outfit. A nigga almost wanted to tell her to go inside and take that shit off, but I didn't. I reached in my pocket and gave her the roll of money. I pulled her close to me and slipped the bag of weed in the waistband of her skirt and pulled her jacket back down to conceal it.

"Hey Juvie, I'm Chunky." He said introducing himself because the shit slipped my mind.

"My bad lil mama that's my nigga Chunky, Chunky this my lil mama Juvie." She spoke back and waved before refocusing her attention on me.

"Thanks baby. You coming by later?"

"Yeah, just hit me up when you get back." I told her pulling her in for a hug. I whispered in her ear, "make sure you keep that skirt on for me when I get back later and them boots too." She giggled but quickly agreed.

"Alright, I'mma see you later let me go handle this lil business." I told her before slipping my tongue in her mouth kissing her. When she opened her eyes, they widened so I turned to see what she was looking at. Chunky stupid ass was staring at us with his mouth wide opened practically drooling. "Let me get this ignant nigga a way from here."

"Whatever nigga." He chuckled.

"See ya later baby, love you."

"Love you too." I told her kissing her once more. It wasn't until she walked off that I noticed the back of her outfit. The back of her jacket had Allen and the number three, and on the back of her skirt written across her ass was Iverson.

"Allen Iverson!" Chunky blurted out and I mugged him so fucking hard.

With each step she took the I and the S jiggled. I definitely wanted to go snatch her ass up now and make her take that shit off but I'm not that kinda nigga. Besides, Juvie can handle herself and with her I never have to question her loyalty.

"Nigga what the fuck, you over there in la-la land, why we still sitting here?" He asked interrupting my trip down memory lane.

"Shut up fool." I said finally backing out of his driveway.

"Well, the good thing is you're not breathing out your ears and eating through a tube."

"The fuck you talking about?"

"Shit she must've not told her daddy yet, since you're still in one piece." Yeah, let me hurry up and go take this nigga to pick up his truck before he get on my fucking nerves, I thought as I drove him to the dealership. After dropping Chunky off it was me alone in my truck again with just my thoughts.

Six months and a day, one hundred eighty-three days, four thousand, three hundred ninety hours, two hundred sixty-three thousand, five hundred twenty minutes, or fifteen million, eight hundred and eleven thousand, two hundred seconds no matter how you count it up it still equals too damn long since I've seen and talked to my Juvie. I've called, texted, and went by her crib but she won't answer. A nigga even went up to her job and they told me she was on leave; shit I even rode by her mom's house just to see if she was there.

I knew I had fucked up by not telling her the truth but shit I didn't think it would come to this. A nigga ain't never felt no heartache like this before. I tried to talk to mama about it and she told me she doesn't feel sorry for me because I did exactly what she told me not to do and that was hurt Juvie. I've been trying to come up with a solution to get my girl back at this point whatever she asks of me I'm willing to do. My life hasn't been the same without her and I can't take this shit anymore. I call her daily, multiple times a day, and it just goes to voicemail, but I can't even leave a message cause it's full and I'm a million percent sure all of the messages are mine.

A nigga so stressed behind losing Juvie and then having to deal with Miranda's bullshit all I do is work, hustle, drink, and smoke weed day in and day out. My house is damn near a battlefield and I'm bout ready to end this shit. Then the bitch be thinking she being sneaky like I'm just some dumb ass nigga and not paying attention to the fact that she leaves home early, comes in late, cooks even less, and on her off days fall of the face of the earth. I don't even care what the fuck she got going on as long as my kids ain't round no random niggas she can do her thug thang.

It was still kinda early and I wasn't ready to go home yet so I decided to go to Sha La. Sha La was a lil lowkey club that catered to an older crowd and was a nice lil chill spot. Sha La, named after its owner, was laid back just like him. So, that's where I was headed or so I thought. My phone rang and seeing Slugga's name definitely raised a red flag, especially since he never hit me on my personal line. I ignored the call at first but when he called right back, I got a gut feeling that I needed to answer that call.

"Sup nigga, the fuck you calling me on this line for." I gritted just in case he was calling about business and called this number by mistake.

"I know what you thinking and it's not like that OG."

"Well, what's up?"

"I don't even know how to come out and say this shit to you." My antennas were definitely all the way up. "As a man I pride myself on minding my own business, but I fucks with you the long way and I just can't let you be blind-sided like that especially with your kids involved."

"The fuck you talking about. What's wrong with my kids?"

"Your kids are good, but you need to get to LaDonna's house as fast you can because there is something you need to see." Not bothering to hear anything else, I turned my truck around and did the dash to Miranda's sister LaDonna's house in St. Gabriel. My mind was racing, and my heart was beating out of my chest as I aimlessly drove trying to get to my kids.

When I finally made it to LaDonna's I didn't see anything out of the ordinary just LaDonna's car, Miranda's truck, and a Chevrolet Silverado who I figured belonged to somebody LaDonna knew. I parked and hopped out, speed walking up the few steps that led to her porch. I knocked loudly waiting for someone to answer the door.

Her sister answered and I didn't miss the widening of her eyes nor the shocked expression on her face seeing it was me. "Lynx what are you doing here?" She practically screamed her question as if I wasn't standing in her face and I thought that shit was strange as fuck.

"Where are my kids?" I asked her.

"They're in the room playing.

"I need to lay eyes on my kids." I told her inviting myself in and going down the hall to the den where the kids usually play whenever we come here. When I opened the door, I got the shock of my life as the wind was knocked completely out of me. On the couch was Miranda and some nigga I ain't never seen before. LuLu was on the floor playing with some toys and LJ was sitting so close to the nigga he was practically in his skin.

"The fuck going on in here?" I spoke up and Miranda's ass froze in place.

"Sup dad? We just watching a movie with my daddy."

"What did you just say?" I asked LJ again because I wanted to make sure what I was seeing and what I heard was correct. He was about to repeat it when Miranda cut her eyes at him instantly silencing him.

"Lynx it ain't what you think." Miranda spoke but I wasn't even listening to her. I was still focused on what caught my eye when I first walked in the room along with what LJ said. Granted I have never thought LJ looked like me everybody always said he resembled her more, but I be damned if LJ didn't look like a perfect blend of Miranda and the nigga sitting next to her.

"LJ, I want you to tell me who this is you're sitting next to ok son. I promise you're not in trouble." He looked at the nigga, he looked at Miranda, he looked at me, and was about to speak when the nigga interrupted him.

"Man, fuck all that. Miranda this shit has gone on long enough tell the man the truth or I will." She shook her head while pleading with her eyes for him not to say anything.

"Look bruh, it ain't no easy way to say this shit

but LJ is biologically my son. Miranda and I was messing around at the same time y'all was back in high school. I ended up getting in some trouble and my folks sent me outta town, so she pinned the baby on you. I just found out about him last year and tracked her down so I could find out the truth and be in his life." I didn't even say nothing, I picked LuLu up and walked out of LaDonna's house without saying a word.

I didn't have to worry about Miranda coming behind me and making a scene because she knew better than anyone else when I'm quiet is when you should be worried. Never once did I ever feel the need to question paternity when it came to LJ but shit after seeing and hearing what I saw and heard today Miranda's scandalous ass had definitely got one over on me. I put LuLu in her seat and got behind the wheel, starting my truck up I headed back to Baton Rouge with one destination in mind.

I couldn't even describe how I was feeling at the moment, the old saying *when it rains it pours* could never be truer. LuLu was so oblivious to what was going on around her then it hit me, she had my daughter around this random ass nigga. My knuckles were white as I gripped the steering wheel angry as hell. My emotions were starting to seep out and I needed to get them under control because for one, my baby girl was in the truck with me and two, I didn't need to have an accident.

It took me about forty-five minutes to reach my destination. I took a deep breath before exhaling because I didn't know how this would turn out. I got out and went around to grab LuLu who had fallen asleep. After locking up my truck I walked to a familiar place, praying for the chance to see a familiar face, and to be greeted with a warm embrace.

BE WITHOUT YOU

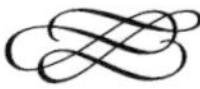

EUPHORIA GUIDRY

March 12,2005

"Friend, you need to make a doctor's appointment. You have been nauseous for almost two weeks now, not keeping anything down, burning up with fever, and that's not good." Rissa was trying to convince me to go to the doctor once again.

"I'm not going to the doctor for them to tell me I have the flu." I groaned out in agony.

"Get dressed, if you're not gonna make an appointment I'm taking you the emergency room. You've even lost weight; it has to be something more than the flu."

"If I go, will you quit bothering me so I can sleep?"

"I promise when we get back you won't hear a peep from me."

I got up and went in the bathroom to take a shower and take care of my hygiene. I caught a glimpse of myself in the mirror and was almost scared of my own damn reflection. Shit, Rissa was right I have lost weight I said taking notice of my appearance.

After I was done in the shower, I moisturized my skin and

brushed my hair into a bun before going back into my room. I got dressed in some sweatpants, t-shirt, a hoodie, socks, and some Nike slippers. I grabbed my purse and phone making my way downstairs so Rissa could take me to the hospital.

"What hospital you wanna go to?" She asked once we were in her car.

"Baton Rouge General on Bluebonnet." I responded while putting my seatbelt on and then reclined the seat.

"Do you want me to call Ms. Karla?"

"Nah, let's see what they say first." I told her before shutting my eyes trying to get a quick nap in before we got there.

It took us about thirty minutes to get there and we found a close parking spot. We walked in and Rissa stood near me as I checked in and came in with me to triage. Next, they sent me to do a urine sample and she waited in the hallway for me. Apparently, my symptoms were serious because they took me straight to the back and put me in a room. I took off my clothes and put the gown on and climbed in bed pulling the covers over me.

"You good friend?" Rissa questioned as I adjusted my body so that I was comfortable.

"Yeah, I'm good."

We had been in the room for about ten minutes when a nurse came in to do bloodwork, swab my throat, and start an IV to give me fluids after informing me that I was severely dehydrated. She told me they were gonna run some tests and the doctor will come in shortly.

Neither Rissa nor myself was prepared for what the doctor would come in to tell me. After asking me a few more questions about my symptoms he scribbled something on his pad. He wanted my permission before speaking in front of Rissa and I told him that it was ok.

"Miss Guidry all of your lab work and tests were negative

except one." The doctor started speaking and I immediately got nervous and broke out in a cold sweat.

"Which one?" I screeched in fear that I had contracted a vicious STD.

"Congratulations you're pregnant!"

I just knew my face had turned Casper the Friendly Ghost white.

"Um err are you sure?" I stuttered out in shock.

"Yes, we did a urine and blood test and they both were positive."

"Then why did I think I have the flu."

"Flu like symptoms or even the flu itself are unusual pregnancy symptoms as well. Do you have any questions for me?"

"No, I don't think so."

"Once you finish this last bag of fluids, I'll discharge you. I recommend you schedule an appointment with your OB/Gyn so you can start your prenatal care. I'll also provide you with pregnancy pamphlets as well. Take care and have a good rest of your evening ladies."

That memory had been embedded in my mind ever since. I never envisioned myself being pregnant and Lynx not being in the picture. Then again, I also never envisioned being pregnant for a married man either. I was able to hide my pregnancy up until mid-April when my baby bump appeared out of nowhere. My dad knew I was pregnant with Lynx's baby, but I lied to my mama and told her I had a one nightstand and ended up pregnant. For some reason I thought it sounded better if she believed I was a whore as opposed to a home wrecker, since she was unaware of my relationship with Lynx before I ended it. Of course, she preached to me about the dangers and risks with having casual and unprotected sex, if only she knew that was far from the truth.

"Friend how long are you gonna keep this up?" Rissa asked interrupting my thoughts with the same question she had asked daily since March 12th.

"Things are fine the way they are."

"E you know this is wrong that man deserves to know about his baby. I know you're still upset about him lying to you but you're basically doing the same thing.

"Don't try to flip the script on me that's not the same thing."

"Friend, you know I'm with ya when ya right, but this is as wrong as two left shoes."

"Think about how hurt you were when you found out his truth, well this is worse because you're robbing him of precious moments that he won't get back. As much as I love going to your appointments with you, I feel that's something Lynx should be there for."

"Oh well, he didn't think about that when he was hiding a damn wife like an Easter egg."

"I think you should at least talk to him and find out why he lied. Be the bigger person and tell him about the baby. Don't force yourself to be a single mother, when you know damn well you don't have to be."

"Rissa, I haven't talked to that man since Christmas. The same night he broke my heart resulting in our relationship's demise. The only good thing about that day was the fact we conceived this baby. How do you even call someone a half a year later and say hey I'm pregnant?"

"You know damn well that man will answer your call on the first ring. The only reason he can't get you on the phone is cause you got it locked away in the damn drawer and he doesn't know you have a new one. That man literally knocked on the door every day for three months straight and still comes by twice a week, and you still won't talk to him."

"I hope that's not your way of pleading his case, cause in the eyes of the law that sounds like some stalker shit."

"Girl boom, I don't know anything about his marriage but clearly you trump that because you seem to be his main focus. Slugga says he asks about you every time he talks to him, and he hates feeling like he's lying to him."

"Tell Slugga it's no different than them pretending not to know each other."

"You are one strong minded ass Taurus. Just think about it friend that's all I ask. I'm praying you do the right thing."

"I hear ya friend, but this is my baby."

"We'll see if you're singing the same tune when I'm at work and you're trying to tend to a baby and study at the same time."

"I will." I smirked as I went in the kitchen to open a jar of pickles.

"Damn baby gonna come out with puckered lips all them damn pickles yo' ass be eating."

"Shut uppppppp!" I laughed at her crazy ass.

"I'll be back I need to run to the hair store. You need anything while I'm out?"

"Nah, I'm good."

"Damn you scared me." I heard Rissa say, which piqued my interest since we were the only ones here which means there was someone at the door when she opened it to leave. I walked as fast as my belly would allow me, to check on my friend.

It seemed as if time stood still when our eyes locked. Lynx was standing in the living room holding a sleeping LuLu. A myriad of emotions flooded through my body as we stared intensely at each other. My eyes betrayed me as tears welled up in the corners of my eyes. There was a magnetic force pulling at the barriers and chains I had securing my heart. His eyes glossed over, and Rissa took LuLu from him laying her on the couch behind him. He took a step closer to me than paused when his eyes finally landed on my swollen belly and his mouth hit the floor.

"Juvie I see you kept your promise." Which caused me to wrinkle my forehead in confusion. "You promised to never kill my seed if you ever ended up pregnant." I nodded through my tears and smiled, because despite it all he didn't even have to question it, he knew for a fact the baby was his.

I moved my feet closing the space in between us and he pulled me into his arms. "You don't know how bad a nigga missed you." He whispered in my ear.

"Y'all are so stinking cute." Rissa squealed as she stood off to the side clapping like a damn proud parent at their kid's award ceremony. She must have hit Jesus on the main line because her prayer was answered quicker than the speed of light. "I'm gonna get out of y'all hair. Byeeee y'all." She waved showing all thirty-two of her teeth before walking out and locking the door behind her.

"Can we talk?" He asked holding my hands out and just taking in my appearance.

"I'd like that let me go get my snacks first. Do you want something to drink?"

"Yeah, juice or a cold drink is good." I fixed him a glass of ice and grabbed a can of Sprite and brought it to him before returning to the kitchen to get my bowl of pickles and my glass of Hawaiian Punch.

All that shit I was talking earlier went clean out the window as I sat next to him on the couch. I so called buried all the feelings and love I had for him while trying to heal from my heartbreak and just like that they had broken free and resurfaced.

"First of all, I wanna apologize to you for not telling you

the truth." He told me with sincerity as he stared into my eyes. "When we first met, I knew there was something about you and I wanted to see what it was, so against my better judgement I withheld that information. As time went on and things got deeper between us, I knew I couldn't tell you and risk losing you but we see how that turned out. I found something in you that I didn't have in the woman I married and for that I don't regret not telling you. My only regret is hurting you and losing the best woman I've ever had."

"I fell so deeply in love with you and thought that there was nothing to ever come between our connection and our bond. The night I asked you that question, I honestly don't know where it came from, but never in a million years did I think you would give me the answer you gave me. That shit shattered my heart and broke me to the core. I stayed locked up in my room until Rissa had enough of my shit."

"Damn! I never meant for none of that to happen. I came back to talk to you later that day, but you wouldn't budge. You was really done with my ass. When I tell you a nigga was sick without you too, Chunky clowned my ass every chance he got, and mama was ready to disown my ass behind you. How far along are you? Do you know what you're having?"

"What's done is done and as bad as it pains me to say this, I can't turn my feelings off for you. I never wanted to be the cause of another woman's hurt. I think we were feeling each other's pain, that's why it was so intense. I'll be twenty-eight weeks tomorrow and it's a boy."

"A boy." He smiled then dropped his head and I couldn't tell if he was excited or disappointed. "Do you need anything? Can I go to your next appointment? I wanna be active in my baby's life and yours too.

"You know what's funny Rissa has been on my ass about

telling you and I wouldn't budge. She was literally just giving me a speech and boom she opens the door and there you were. If I don't know anything else, I know everything happens for a reason. I would love for you to come to my next appointment and be in his life."

"What about your life?"

"Being in his life is being in my life."

"You know what, a nigga mean. I need my Juvie back in my life. I want things to go back to the way they were before you asked me that question."

"I don't wanna be a mistress."

"You never were. I'm more your man than hers."

"Lynx, I don't know. I just can't see myself playing second fiddle to no one."

"When have you ever played second fiddle. I have always made you a priority and her an option."

"So, why not just do the right thing and get a divorce?"

"Shit, it's just cheaper to keep her but no for real I can't because of her." He pointed at LuLu.

"What about her?"

"My baby is too young, and her mama plays too many games as it is. I can't risk something happening to my baby girl and she not being able to tell me all because her mama got her around some random ass nigga." I nodded because I understood where he was coming from.

"If we're gonna do this, it's gonna be on my terms and conditions. For starters, can we just take things slow?"

"It's always been your world, I'm just in it." He pulled me in for a hug and kissed me on my forehead.

My hormones got the best of me and the next thing I know our tongues were dancing around in each other's mouths. "Oh, how I missed this." I thought to myself.

"I missed this too." He said once we had finally pulled away for air. That damn soul tie shit never gets old.

"Come on let's go to my room."

"Juvie, I'm trying to respect your wishes and take it slow but if we go upstairs, a nigga gonna want some of that pregnant pussy."

"We can take it slow afterwards but right now I really need to feel you."

"Your wish is my command." He scooped me up bridal style.

"You better not drop me."

"I got you and my son lil mama."

He carried me upstairs and gently laid me in the center of my bed as he stood stripping out of his clothes. "Damn it just hit me, you said you're twenty-eight weeks that means we made him on Christmas." I nodded my head as I smiled wide at his discovery. "Yeah, this was definitely God's plan."

Lynx climbed in bed and helped me undress until we both was naked as the day we were born. He stared at me taking in every inch of my body as if it was his very first time seeing it. One thing for sure he always made me feel like the most beautiful woman in the world and this time was no different.

"Just put it in." I encouraged him not wanting to waste time with any foreplay, I wanted the dick.

"I got you lil mama." He said pushing my legs apart with my feet planted on the bed. He positioned his head at my entrance and slowly worked it in stretching me out in the process.

"Sssssssss." I hissed. Once he was balls deep, he stroked me long and hard touching my spot with each thrust. "Ooooohhh baby, I missed this dick." I moaned out.

"He missed you too lil mama." He replied before teasing

my nipple with his tongue heightening the pleasure, he was giving me. "You like that Juvie?"

"Yessssssssss baby, it feels so good."

"You want me to stop?"

"Fuck no, please don't stop." I gritted out as my eyes rolled in the back of my head and that familiar wave of pleasure hit me abruptly. "Oh Lynx, I'm about to cum." I managed to get out right before I nutted so hard, I momentarily got lightheaded.

"You wanna get up here and ride your dick?"

"Hell yeah before this belly gets too big and I won't be able to." He pulled out of me and helped me switch positions. I loved how he was always so gentle and attentive with me, and this time was no different.

Lynx laid back, dick hard, and standing tall pointing at the ceiling. I crawled over to him and eased my way onto his stiffness. "You good lil mama?" I nodded and started to ride him slowly rotating my hips just the way he liked it. I was gripping the dick with my pussy, and he was massaging my titties with his hands.

"Fuck Juvie a nigga bout to bust." Mission accomplished after my first nut I was ready to curl up and go to sleep, but I couldn't leave him unsatisfied. I continued to ride slightly raising up off the dick and slamming down on it tightening my pussy muscles around his dick each time. A few moments later his was warm cum filled my pussy up and I collapsed on his chest. "I love you Juvie."

"I love you too, baby." Once our breathing had returned to normal, he gently laid me on my side as he got up to go clean himself off and cleaned me up immediately after. We both got dressed and went back downstairs to check on LuLu who was still sleeping, so I covered her up with the throw blanket I brought down with me. We settled on the couch continuing our conversation as I finally ate my pickles.

"You know I quit UPS?"

"I remember you telling me you were thinking about quitting, so you finally did it huh?"

"Yeah, I started driving for Budweiser at the end of January."

"That's good, you like it?"

"Yeah, the hours, pay, and benefits are all better."

"I'm so happy for you."

"For me, baby this is for us."

Time was flying, it started to get late, and he needed to get LuLu home. He picked her up and walked over to the door and I walked behind him opening the door he stepped out kissing me.

"For the record, you're not the cause of another woman's pain, she just has the title of being my wife. Our marriage was in shambles long before you came into the picture, and you came in and filled the missing void in my life simply by being you. You're honestly my first love, you got a nigga heart, we got a bond that's so deep we couldn't permanently sever that shit if we tried, and now you're carrying my first-born son. Fuck a title, our bond carries more weight."

"First-born son." I repeated in confusion. "What about LJ?"

"I found out today he isn't mine." He choked out damn near in tears.

TO BE CONTINUED

To Be Continued

Made in United States
Orlando, FL
02 May 2023

32709995R00098